THE TEX...

All the news th...

Fortune Heir Charged With Murder!

Red Rock is all abuzz with the news that Sheriff Wyatt Grayhawk has charged Jonas Goodfellow with the murder of *their* uncle, Ryan Fortune. It appears that this importer deliberately gave a poisoned bottle of port wine to the Fortune family's patriarch at the recent bash to welcome the lost heirs.

But the burning question on everyone's mind is—who's that pretty young blonde who posted his bail money and has been by his side ever since?

That "pretty young blonde" is Jonas's loyal assistant, Tara Summers. Ms. Summers flew from their global headquarters in San Francisco to open a satellite office in town, since Jonas can't leave Red Rock until the charges are dropped. Our sources tell us the pair is sharing a suite at a local hotel, but from the looks they've been secretly exchanging, Jonas may have just leapt from the frying pan...into the fire!

Dear Reader,

Welcome to Silhouette Desire, where every month you'll find six passionate, powerful and provocative romances.

October's MAN OF THE MONTH is *The Taming of Jackson Cade*, part of bestselling author BJ James' MEN OF BELLE TERRE miniseries, in which a tough horse breeder is gentled by a lovely veterinarian. *The Texan's Tiny Secret* by Peggy Moreland tells the moving story of a woman in love with the governor of Texas and afraid her scandalous past will hurt him.

The exciting series 20 AMBER COURT continues with Katherine Garbera's *Some Kind of Incredible,* in which a secretary teaches her lone-wolf boss to take a chance on love. In *Her Boss's Baby,* Cathleen Galitz's contribution to FORTUNES OF TEXAS: THE LOST HEIRS, a businessman falsely accused of a crime finds help from his faithful assistant and solace in her virginal embrace.

Jacob's Proposal, the first book in Eileen Wilks' dynamic new series, TALL, DARK & ELIGIBLE, features a marriage of convenience between a beauty and a devastatingly handsome financier known as the Iceman. And Maureen Child's popular BACHELOR BATTALION marches on with *Last Virgin in California,* an opposites-attract romance between a tough, by-the-book marine drill instructor and a free-spirited heroine.

So celebrate the arrival of autumn by indulging yourself with all six of these not-to-be-missed love stories.

Enjoy!

Joan Marlow Golan

Joan Marlow Golan
Senior Editor, Silhouette Desire

Please address questions and book requests to:
Silhouette Reader Service
U.S.: 3010 Walden Ave., P.O. Box 1325, Buffalo, NY 14269
Canadian: P.O. Box 609, Fort Erie, Ont. L2A 5X3

Her Boss's Baby
CATHLEEN GALITZ

Published by Silhouette Books
America's Publisher of Contemporary Romance

Special thanks and acknowledgment are given
to Cathleen Galitz for her contribution to
THE FORTUNES OF TEXAS: THE LOST HEIRS series.

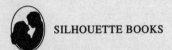 SILHOUETTE BOOKS

ISBN 0-373-76396-4

HER BOSS'S BABY

Visit Silhouette at www.eHarlequin.com

Printed in U.S.A.

Books by Cathleen Galitz

Silhouette Desire

The Cowboy Takes a Bride #1271
Wyoming Cinderella #1373
Her Boss's Baby #1396

Silhouette Romance

The Cowboy Who Broke the Mold #1257
100% Pure Cowboy #1279
Wyoming Born & Bred #1382

CATHLEEN GALITZ,

a Wyoming native, teaches English to seventh to twelfth graders in a rural school that houses kindergartners and seniors in the same building. She lives in a small Wyoming town with her husband and two children. When she's not busy writing, teaching or working with her Cub Scout den, she can most often be found hiking or snowmobiling in the Wind River Mountains.

 Meet the Fortunes of Texas

*Meet the Fortunes of Texas's Lost Heirs—membership in
this Texas family has its privileges and its price. As the
family gathers to welcome its newest members, it discovers
a murderer in its midst...and passionate new romances
that only a true-bred Texas love can bring!*

CAST OF CHARACTERS

Jonas Goodfellow: Falsely arrested for Ryan Fortune's
murder, this lost heir wants nothing more to do with that
nest of vipers he'd foolishly hoped would accept him as
kith and kin.

Tara Summers: From the day he gave this inexperienced
high school graduate her first job, she's been in love with
her boss. But now that she's pregnant with the boss's baby,
is Jonas about to promote her to...wife?

Ryan Fortune: Having faced his own mortality, the family
patriarch now has some special gifts in mind for four
people who saw him through his darkest hour....

One

Tara Summers smoothed out the nonexistent wrinkles in the fashionable pink power suit she had chosen expressly for the occasion. Aware that she was the focus of attention in the front office of the small jailhouse, she couldn't help fretting if her skirt wasn't a tad too short. She had picked out this particular outfit hoping it would make her feel both professional and sexy. From the head-to-toe ogling she was receiving from the officers on duty, it appeared she had achieved at least one of the two desired effects.

If only Jonas thinks so, she agonized, worrying her lower lip between her teeth.

The irony of the situation did not escape her. Five years ago the tables had been turned, and it had been Jonas Goodfellow who had arrived like a chivalrous knight of old to bail her and his kid stepsister out of jail. Only seventeen at the time, Tara had been mor-

tified when she and Ellen had been incarcerated for a
drinking violation following their high-school gradu-
ation. Still green around the gills, she had burst into
tears at the first inclination that Jonas was about to
administer a well-deserved tongue-lashing.

Between sobs she'd explained the reason for her
unprecedented behavior. She desperately needed a job
to support her ailing widowed father. At her age without a college degree or experience in anything other
than part-time waitressing, life appeared hopeless.

Moved by her plight, Jonas wiped away her tears
with his handkerchief and offered her a job on the
spot. He was just starting up his own business and
said he could use someone to mind the store and answer the phone when he was out of the country. Starting pay was more than Tara could have expected anywhere else. Not only would it help salvage her
father's dignity, the money would allow her to take a
couple of college classes at night, as well.

"You'll never regret it," she promised him, grate-
fully pumping his hand like a well-oiled piston.

A pair of twinkling green eyes and a wicked smile
pulled Tara back into the present. "Are you sure that
a sweet young thing like yourself really wants to bail
out an attempted murderer—considering the fact that
you could be spending your time with an upright
good-looking fellow such as myself?"

The police officer behind the desk threw out his
chest to add to the appeal of his offer. He seemed
nice, close to her own age and charming in a boyishly
cute way. Just the sort of all-American guy her father
was always after her to date. He often reminded her
how much he wanted a couple more grandkids to
bounce on his knee.

Tara took a deep breath before replying, "I'm positive. Now will you please take me to see Jonas?"

Regardless of how bad things looked, she wasn't about to abandon Jonas now. This was her big chance to pay him back for his kindness and generosity. And to prove that she was no longer the girl he'd rescued so long ago.

Goosebumps raised along the length of her arms as Tara followed the officer through the office into the jail itself. She wasn't sure whether to attribute them to the sudden drop in temperature or the chilling atmosphere of the dismal holding area. Tara squinted in the harsh light, looking past rows of steel bars.

Who is that unshaven man sitting on the edge of his cot, holding his head in his hands? Surely not clean-cut, always in control, take-charge-of-the-world Jonas Goodfellow.

Reminding herself that he couldn't be expected to be at his charming best, Tara tried touching him gently with her smile.

Awakened from his melancholic stupor by the subtle scent of her perfume, Jonas raised his head. Blue eyes collided with brown, and a frisson of electrical energy melted the bars that separated them, creating the illusion that they were the only two people on earth.

Who is that angel in pink? Jonas wondered. *Surely not that scared high-school graduate I hired to answer phones for me just a couple of short years ago.*

Indeed not. This was a woman, mature in both mind and body. A woman who knew full well the effect she was having on every male in the joint. How amazing, it must seem to them, that a model could

walk off of the pages of a glossy fashion magazine
and into their collective fantasies.

Jonas groaned. It was hard enough defending a
lady's honor when one wasn't behind bars. A low
whistle emanating from the cell directly across the
way confirmed his worst fears. Accompanying suggestions turned the lady in question the same lovely
shade of pink as her suit. The stern reprimand that
the young police cadet in charge issued was met by
guffaws.

Never in all his life had Jonas wanted to bash in
someone's head as badly as he did at this very moment. Humiliation and indignation were powerful
stimulants when mixed in a vial already overflowing
with injustice. Seeing Tara's smile wobble, he
growled at his fellow prisoner, "It's a good thing
you're penned up way over there. Otherwise I'd wa-
ger you'd have trouble trying to whistle without any
teeth."

In response, the other man flung a filthy string of
expletives in his direction. He also took a step away
from the bars to make sure he was out of reach when
the officer unlocked Jonas's cell.

Jonas regretted Tara's seeing him like this. Had he
anyone else in the world to call upon, he would have
spared his lovely young secretary the trip from San
Francisco to the boondocks of Texas. Unfortunately
Jonas had no family left except his stepfather and
stepsister, Ellen, who was expecting a baby anytime
now. Considering her delicate condition, he didn't
want to put any extra strain on her. And Jonas would
have preferred death in the electric chair than to ask
his stepfather for a favor. Not that asking would have
made any difference. Nicolas Goodfellow would re-

fuse to help. Just as surely as he had refused to have anything to do with raising Jonas or caring for his needy young wife, who had meekly submitted to his emotional abuse right up until the day she died.

"Thanks for coming," Jonas said to Tara as the door to his cell swung open. "You're certainly a sight for sore eyes."

Though he resisted the urge to give her an appreciative hug in front of their watchful audience, she was not given to such reserve. Wrapping her arms around him, she brushed a kiss across his stubbled cheek, causing yet another crude comment to bubble up from the gutter of another captive's mind.

For all the times Jonas had imagined holding this woman in his arms, he couldn't believe how good she felt. Way too good. For the hundredth time, he had to remind himself that theirs was an employee/employer relationship. Friendly and respectful. Anything more would be taking advantage of Tara's sweet nature and naiveté.

"Let's get you out of here," she whispered in his ear.

The sensation of her breath on his neck caused Jonas's skin to tingle. What was that scent she was wearing? A heady mixture of flowers and musk, it was an importer's dream. Jonas was certain he could sell gallons of the stuff.

After almost three days of confinement, he was eager to leave the premises. Happy to let Tara lead the way, he couldn't help but notice the way the young officer's gaze lingered on the hypnotic swaying of her hips. Jonas's chest tightened uncomfortably. He tried brushing the feeling off as the onset of bronchial pneumonia that he'd likely contracted from one of the

thugs with whom he'd been forced to share quarters
for the past fifty-six hours and twenty-two minutes.

Not that he was counting.

Jonas said a little prayer of thanksgiving as he entered the light of freedom. Relative freedom, he
amended, cursing the fact that for the time being the
bail money Tara had procured from the business lib-
erated him only from his cell. Unless the charges
against him were dropped, Jonas would be required
to remain in the tightly knit community of Red Rock
until the time of his trial. As far as he could tell, the
small town existed for the sole purpose of servicing
the Fortune family—that nest of vipers that he had so
foolishly hoped would welcome him as kith and kin.

He was charged with the attempted murder of one
of the town's most prominent citizens. The fact that,
as far as Jonas could tell, everyone in Red Rock, from
the local pharmacist to the sheriff, was related only
made matters that much worse. He figured he'd been
lucky not to have been lynched while he awaited bail.
He'd be even luckier to get out of town in one piece.
One thing was for certain. Good old Sheriff Grayhawk wasn't about to risk upsetting his pretty little
wife by letting anyone off the hook who was even
circumstantially implicated in harming her favorite
uncle.

To the lawman's credit, however, Grayhawk hadn't
gone out of his way to persecute him. Fortunately it
appeared the sheriff was more into justice than pun-
ishment. Still, given the hostile stares leveled at him
by both employees and visitors as he left the county
building, Jonas was certain he would be under careful
surveillance as long as he remained in Grayhawk's
jurisdiction.

Stepping outside into the bright light of a Texas summer day, he realized just how much he had taken such a simple pleasure for granted: the warmth of the sun and of Tara's smile. The way the light caught in her blond hair, which tumbled about her shoulders in an aura of golden diffusion, almost made him question for a moment whether she was wearing a halo. A telltale shiver told Jonas just how relieved this angel was to be well out of such an awful place.

"I can't begin to tell you how much I appreciate you coming to bail me out," he began stiffly.

Knowing how Jonas hated being indebted to anyone, Tara would have none of it. "You'd do the same for me," she assured him with a blinding smile. "In fact, I believe you already have."

"It's hardly the same," he retorted bitterly.

"Of course it is," she insisted. "It's my turn to take care of you now."

Though Jonas looked genuinely insulted by the thought, Tara felt certain his masculine pride would ultimately take a back seat to his gratitude. At least she hoped so as she directed him toward the car she had rented for the length of their stay in Red Rock.

Feminine instinct compelled her to toss him the keys. Having worked so closely with this man for the past five years, she had absolutely no fear that he would do anything as foolish as attempt to bolt from town. She smiled at him as he opened her car door. Even under the most dire of circumstances, she could always count on Jonas to be a gentleman. It was one of the things she found most endearing about him.

Tara filled him in on the arrangements she had made as they drove to the hotel where they would be staying until this whole mess was cleared up. As always, Jonas was impressed with his assistant's efficiency. He may have initially taken her under his wing out of pity, but the truth of the matter was that hiring Tara Summers was the smartest business move he'd ever made. Again he forced himself to remember just how foolish it would be to jeopardize such a remarkable working relationship by doing anything as stupid as pulling over to the side of the road and kissing her senseless. After all, someone as moral and inexperienced as Tara might mistake such purely masculine impulsiveness as being something far more than it actually was: lust and appreciation wrapped up in one hormonally charged package.

"It's far from perfect, but it's the best I could do on such short notice," she said, needlessly apologizing for the arrangements she'd made to procure for him the only official suite in the small town. "I've had all the necessary equipment to run the business long distance shipped here. Everything should be here by tomorrow."

A blush crept up her neckline as she explained in a rush how two separate bedrooms adjoined a relatively spacious central living area that would have to serve as their temporary office "until this little matter gets cleared up."

"Always the master of understatement," Jonas quipped, pulling up in front of the hotel.

As grateful as he was that Tara had taken all necessary precautions to keep his mind off the gravity of his situation, it bothered Jonas that she seemed so unsettled by the thought of sharing close quarters with him. Didn't she trust him enough to keep his hands to himself?

Switching off the ignition, he leaned across the

seat. Tipping up her chin to force her to make eye contact with him, he asked her point-blank, "What are you afraid of, little one? Haven't I always been a perfect gentleman around you?"

That's the problem! she longed to tell him, melting at the endearment designed to remind her of the difference in their ages. *What I'm really afraid of is that you have absolutely no interest in me as a woman. A woman who wants to be more to you than just a loyal employee.*

But there was no way she could tell him that, not when she was in the process of falling headlong into a pair of eyes so blue that she was certain it would be impossible to hide any falsehood there. Surely if he was guilty of any wrongdoing, she would be able to discern it just by looking into those eyes. At the mere touch of his thumb beneath her chin, Tara felt the familiar jolt of electricity that tugged at her insides and made mush of rational thought every time he came in physical contact with her.

Don't you feel it, too? she wanted to ask.

Remembering some of the late nights they had spent working overtime when she had caught him looking at her as more than a mere employee, Tara was certain he must. Ever the gentleman, however, he had never acted on the predatory desire she had seen in those electric blue eyes. And he never would, she feared, unless she gave him some blatant encouragement. A pretty new dress and expensive perfume were too subtle by themselves.

Brazenly she traced the outline of his jaw with her index finger. If anything, she thought that two-day stubble and haunted look in his eyes only made him more outrageously masculine than ever. Indeed, such a rebel could capture any woman's heart with a single glance.

"Has it ever occurred to you that maybe you're the one who has something to fear?" Tara asked in a squeaky voice she barely recognized as her own.

The deep bass tones of Jonas's laughter filled the car. Clearly uncomfortable with the direction this conversation was taking, he seized Tara's hand to try to stop her from making an even bigger fool of herself. Putting her hand demurely back into her own lap, he threw in one of his patented winks in hopes of keeping the mood light.

"Just in case you're tempted to play with fire, I promise to keep *my* door locked. I'm already in enough trouble without being accused of robbing the cradle, too."

Two

Seething at the flippancy of Jonas's comment, Tara held her head high as they checked into the hotel. The twelve years separating them were hardly enough to put her thirty-four-year-old boss over the hill. It wasn't as if he was old enough to be her father or that anyone could mistake her for a teenager. Tara's feminine pride was assuaged somewhat by the elderly desk clerk's arched eyebrow at two unmarried people signing in for a single suite. Obviously *he* didn't think she was too young for Jonas.

"I'll remind you that we're a respectable establishment," the older man said sanctimoniously as he passed them a set of keys.

Jonas glared at him but declined to explain the situation. The old duffer would probably have a connip- tion fit when he realized an accused murderer was staying under his inviolable roof, he thought as he opened the door to the suite.

The hotel was the best Red Rock had to offer. Decorated in muted mauve and turquoise Southwestern designs, the suite had an air of fading elegance. The living room was spacious enough to make-do as a temporary office, though Jonas suspected it would get crowded once all the equipment and paperwork arrived. Over Tara's objections, he insisted she take the roomier master bedroom, which had a view of a picturesque city park. As long as his room had a bed and a telephone, Jonas was set. After spending the past couple of nights sleeping on a cot under a scratchy blanket, he assured her this was near heaven.

"I hope you don't mind that I took the liberty of bringing along some of your personal items," Tara said, producing the shaving kit he kept at the office as a spare.

Jonas could have kissed her. The idea flitted through his mind like a golden butterfly canvasing a field of flowers. Instantly he squashed the impulse.

Running his hand over the stubble on his chin, he told Tara how much he appreciated her thoughtfulness. "You know how I hate feeling scruffy."

All Tara knew was that she wouldn't mind getting a whisker rub from this blue-eyed demon. As she set about unpacking her own things, she took decided comfort in the buzz of the electric razor starting up in the bathroom. It was the kind of everyday soothing sound to which she could definitely grow accustomed. Absently she wondered if married couples truly appreciated such simple joys of cohabitation.

When Tara heard the shower being turned on, she marveled at how the thought of such an ordinary hygienic act could bring sweat to her brow. All she could think of was the close proximity of Jonas, naked. The water caressing his six-foot-three body, his glistening muscles, and...

Ten minutes later he emerged from the bathroom wearing nothing but a thick towel wrapped around his middle. With his dark hair shimmering with water, he looked every bit a Roman gladiator. It was all Tara could do to refrain from asking if he would like help wiping that spot on his broad shoulders that he had missed.

"You look like a nude man," she said with a smile, then realizing the embarrassing Freudian slip, tripped all over her tongue trying to correct herself. "A new man! I meant to say you look like a new man."

The sound of Jonas's laughter washed over her. He did have a wonderful way of putting her at ease in the most difficult of moments.

"Listen," he said with a lopsided smile, "I know how awkward this has to be for you. I'll promise to try to stay out of your way if you'll do the same for me. I apologize for my state of undress, too, but I'm actually thinking of burning the clothes I was wearing. I don't want anything around to remind me of the time I spent in that jail cell. Being the superefficient assistant that you are, I was hoping you might have brought me a couple of clean things to wear..."

Once again on firmer ground, Tara hastened to make him forget her earlier blunder. "I already put clean clothes on your bed. I didn't bring much along because I figured it would be just as easy to buy a few things while we're here. You know I've been wanting to update your wardrobe for quite some time now."

Jonas inserted an injured tone to his voice. "Just be forewarned I'm not about to get a nose ring to go along with any trendy clothes you pick out to bring me into the new millennium."

It was the kind of warm funny banter that Tara liked to think might someday be a part of their marriage. As much as Jonas would like to dismiss her as nothing more than an employee, she couldn't keep waiting for him to notice she'd grown up. She was, after all, far too bright and ambitious to remain at a dead-end job forever. Certain that this was the perfect opportunity for her to prove what a wonderful wife she would make him, Tara had every intention of maximizing their time together.

"Remind me to give you a raise," Jonas said, padding off in the direction of his bedroom. "You take awfully good care of me."

"I'd sure like to," she replied softly to a backside that made her suck in her breath with longing.

Seeing the damp imprints of his feet across the plush carpet, she wondered if marriages really did break up over such inconsequential things as a husband failing to dry his feet or replace the roll of toilet paper or squeeze the toothpaste from the bottom. Tara had read articles about such things, but found the idea preposterous. She sighed deeply. Only time would tell whether close proximity would indeed bring her closer to the man she wanted—or if it would drive them apart.

Tara knew that some women would be offended by Jonas's expectations of her as an employee. She understood that it was her duty as a modern woman to rage against any request to make coffee or pick up dry cleaning or, say, pack up the office and move it to Dust Blown, Texas. But she just couldn't muster up much indignation. Love had a way of making the most mundane chores a joy.

Aside from the fact that she enjoyed being near Jonas, Tara knew she was well compensated, financially, for what she did. And with a little luck she had every intention of moving up in his affections.

She also knew that self-reliant Jonas was likely to do everything in his power to keep her at arm's length. It clearly amused him how she blushed or trembled whenever he came too close. A less-determined woman might have given up on having anything more than a platonic relationship with him. Not Tara Summers. Having supported both herself and her father ever since she was seventeen, she knew what the word *persistence* really meant. This was her chance to pay Jonas back for having faith in her when nobody else had and to finally make her feelings known. If she couldn't muster up the courage here, she knew it wouldn't happen back in San Francisco, where they would no doubt fall back into the same old productive platonic patterns of behavior.

A virgin, Tara felt a certain amount of trepidation—and a good deal of anticipation—at the prospect of spending a prolonged period of time in confined quarters with such a sexy virile man. But at the ripe old age of twenty-two, she was past caring about what damage could be done to her reputation.

In fact, she was pretty sure her virginity was her reputation.

Not that she hadn't had any chances, romantically speaking. Plenty of men had made plays for her, but an old-fashioned girl at heart, Tara was hoping to share the gift of herself with a man who truly loved her. A man who she loved with the kind of passion immortalized in the tender verses she so esteemed. Certainly Jonas's was as tragic a story as any the great bard had imagined. Although she knew he didn't blame her for the predicament in which he found himself, Tara couldn't help feeling guilty for the part she had played in getting him to come to Texas.

When he returned to the living room a moment later, Jonas was wearing a new pair of khaki pants and a soft white polo shirt. She was in the midst of deciding whether she liked him more as a rough-shaven rebel or a clean-shaven jock when it occurred to her that he really fit into neither category. One minute he was looking right into her soul with those piercing eyes and the very next moment his eyes would soften to reveal the hint of a little boy all alone against the world.

"Are you ready to fill me in on what's happened?" she asked, taking a soda from the wet bar and offering him one, as well.

"After all I've been through, I think I deserve something stronger," Jonas told her, settling down into a sofa and stretching his long legs across the expanse of velvet striping.

Tara substituted a beer for the pop and handed it to him. Then she draped her jacket on the back of her chair.

Noticing the wonders her feminine curves did for the simple scoop-neck shell and matching skirt she wore, Jonas took a long swig of his drink before beginning. "Well, of course, you know all about how I ended up here in the first place."

"The invitation," she supplied, feeling a twinge of culpability for her part in encouraging him to come to the Double Crown Ranch. Loyally tied to her own family, she had been thrilled when Jonas told her about the invitation he'd received several months ago from his long-lost uncle, Ryan Fortune, asking him to attend a reunion party for his sister and brother's "lost heirs." Apparently, good-looking smooth-talking Cameron Fortune had numerous affairs during his marriage and managed to father three illegitimate children before he was killed in a car crash—with his young assistant.

Jonas's initial reaction was to scorn the invitation outright. After all, the only thing his birth father had ever given him was a start in the womb of a woman who deserved a whole lot better than she ever got. The thought of that dear woman having to endure Nicolas Goodfellow's emotional abuse just to secure her illegitimate child a name and a trim suburban home was more than Jonas's heart could bear considering even now. Other than the fact that it would have given him a good deal of satisfaction to look Cameron up one day and spit in his face, he wasn't particularly sorry that his biological father was dead.

Still, Ryan Fortune had sounded so genuinely nice over the phone, trying to right his older brother's wrongs, that Jonas had been sorely tempted to connect with the family he'd never known he had. Since his mother had passed away four years ago, Jonas knew any action he took couldn't harm her in any way.

And he had been curious, after all.

For years he'd wondered about the man who had abandoned his mother. The one time he had probed for answers, she had bitterly referred to his conception as the product of her only one-night stand. Embarrassed, her ultra-strict religious parents had refused to have anything more to do with her. Shame still burned in her pale gaunt cheeks as she recalled those dismal days, trying to make it all on her own on minimum-wage shift work. That it turned out that Jonas's real daddy was a multimillionaire didn't make him any more palatable to the child he'd deserted.

The fact that a stray dog would have gotten better treatment than Jonas had at the hands of his stepfather made his accomplishments all that much more impressive. That he had been able to make something of himself despite all odds was perhaps the biggest reason for him to succumb to the urge to seek out his roots. Many people would clamor to meet their rich relatives in hopes of ingratiating themselves and asking for money; Jonas preferred to let the Fortunes know he didn't want a damned thing from them.

Other than the respect he'd been denied from birth.

"I brought along a bottle of wine to the reunion like you suggested," Jonas continued, methodically explaining the events that led him to jail. "As a gesture of goodwill."

Tara nodded. She knew he wasn't attaching any guilt to her well-intended idea.

"From that special French shipment. Yes, I remember," she said.

"It was well received." Jonas paused thoughtfully before adding almost as an afterthought. "As was I."

Knowing how much it would please her, he considered telling her how good it had felt being instantly accepted into the Fortune family. They all seemed to be such lovely people—on the surface. After years of enduring his stepfather's emphatic declarations that he was most definitely not of his loins, Jonas thought he had finally found home.

That home was a Spanish-style mansion situated in the midst of the untold number of acres constituting the fabulous Double Crown Ranch. But this was not nearly as important to Jonas as the fact that such benevolent successful people seemed so anxious to claim him as their own.

"Was there a problem with the wine?" Tara prodded, obviously unaware of the lump lodged like a fist in Jonas's throat at the memory.

"You could say that," he replied, the corners of his mouth turning up wryly at the corners at the understatement. There was no tactful way to break the news to her. "Shortly afterward, my uncle was admitted to the hospital, and that particular bottle of wine tested positive for poison. Hence, in a nutshell, my unfortunate incarceration."

Tara gasped in disbelief. It had never occurred to her that when she encouraged Jonas to establish ties with the Fortunes, there would be even the slightest chance he would be implicated in any kind of criminal activity. Certainly nothing as heinous as what he had just relayed.

The tortured look in those cerulean eyes almost doubled Tara over in empathy. She rushed to his defense in a sputter of denouncement. "But there's absolutely nothing wrong with that wine! Despite the extravagant price, it's one of our most popular sellers. In fact, I put in another order to France just two days ago. If there was anything wrong, I'm sure it would have been recalled by the company."

Surprised by her naiveté in assuming the wine had been tampered with at the factory, Jonas assured her,

"Just to be safe, let's pull all remaining cases from the showroom floor. I've insisted that the police test the bottle itself. Seeing how I was eager to make a good first impression, I splurged and bought a big bottle, more than could fit into the antique cut-glass decanter that Ryan poured it into."

"Even if it tests positive," Tara declared implacably, "I don't see how they can possibly tie the crime to you. It isn't like you were the only guest at the reunion."

Her outrage was gratifying. In a dark secret part of his heart, Jonas had been bracing himself for the possibility that she might jump to the same conclusion the police had: that he was guilty of attempted murder. Not only was he personally tied to the murder weapon, Sheriff Grayhawk had been quick to point out how easy it would have been for Jonas, as an international importer, to illegally obtain the digitalis without a prescription from an overseas supplier. All things considered, even his high-priced lawyer admitted that the outlook for Jonas wasn't bright.

It would have killed him to have spied either fear or reproach in his assistant's big brown eyes. Though he knew he was far from a knight in shining armor, that Tara held him in such openly high regard made Jonas want to be a better man. Maybe he wasn't worthy of being up on that pedestal where Tara had put him, but he wasn't ready to relinquish the position just yet.

He was quick to agree with her assessment of the situation. "Of course you're right. What with Storm Pearce, one of the other two lost heirs, in addition to Uncle Ryan and Aunt Miranda, there had to be enough Fortune cousins and in-laws there to populate at least half of this dusty little town.''

"Surely your uncle realizes that anyone could have—''

"Ryan isn't in the position to do much clear thinking right now. He's still in the hospital, deathly ill. As I understand it, he's not out of the woods yet.''

That particular bombshell lay between them as yet unexploded. If Ryan Fortune were to actually die, Jonas was certain to be charged with his murder. In a state renowned for putting men to death as an example to others, his odds were not good for anything lighter than a life sentence if a jury actually found him guilty by a preponderance of evidence, circumstantial or not.

Things were definitely more serious than Tara had suspected when she had packed up and headed to Texas. She had been under the impression that this was all some sort of gigantic mistake that could easily be cleared up with a little time, logic and detective work.

"But what reason could you possibly have for wanting to kill your uncle?'' she demanded to know as if already playing out the courtroom scene in her head.

"Besides the possibility of inheriting millions?'' Jonas supplied with a twisted self-deprecating grin. "According to Sheriff Grayhawk, revenge is always a viable incentive. He's well aware that I've never held my real father in much esteem. He seems to think that animosity could carry over to his brother, my uncle Ryan. As much as I hate to admit it, any qualified psychiatrist could have a field day analyzing my motives.''

Tara's head was swimming. She was glad she wasn't drinking anything stronger than ginger ale. A person needed all her faculties to piece this hodge-podge together. She eyed Jonas's drink suspiciously. "You don't think anyone would tamper with our drinks, do you?"

"I've considered the possibility. Though I wouldn't put it past anyone in Red Rock to try and do me in while I'm holed up here, I think we're safe as long as we check to make sure the containers are properly sealed."

The mere suggestion that Jonas might not get out of town alive sent a shiver up Tara's spine.

"I'd certainly understand if you didn't feel like sticking around," Jonas said, reading the goose bumps on her arms.

"Just try to get rid of me," she quipped with false brightness.

Nothing short of dynamite was going to blast her away from this man's side in his time of need. If anything happened to Jonas, she didn't know how she could continue getting up in the mornings. Whether he knew it or not, he was the center of her universe. Rather than dwelling on any pessimistic possibilities, Tara decided to approach this particular predicament as she did every other problem in her life—one me-thodical step at a time.

Setting her drink down, she signaled that break time was over. She was ready to get back to work.

"As soon as the computer arrives, we'll get online and catch up on correspondence and paperwork. Then we'll set about figuring out who the real criminal in your loving family is and decide how best to go about clearing your name."

The tired smile Jonas gave her was tinged with bitterness. "Goodfellow may be a bastard's name passed down illegitimately, but after all that's happened, I have to admit that I prefer it to the one that's brought me nothing but mis-Fortune since I set foot in Texas."

Three

———

Just watching Tara Summers at work was enough to make most people tired. Jonas likened it to studying the mighty ant in action. Seemingly there was no task too big for her to tackle. So when his assistant calmly announced that she had plans to catch the real criminal and clear his name, Jonas was tempted to call the local law-enforcement agencies and put them on alert.

He placed a hand on her shoulder, foolishly hoping the gesture alone would somehow be enough to stop her. "Listen, Tara, I don't want you doing anything stupid on my behalf. I'd never forgive myself if anything were to happen to you. As flawed as the system may be, let's put our trust in it and allow the police to do their job. The last thing I need or want is for you to go risking your pretty little neck for me."

Tara felt a tingle on her shoulder where his hand rested. The touch seared her, burning through layers of clothing. Though the use of the word *pretty* was flattering, the statement made her feel like a silly schoolgirl.

"What do I have to do to get you to stop bossing me around like I'm some helpless child?" she asked in exasperation.

Jonas's eyes darkened in response. He'd been having a heck of a time seeing her as an ingenue for quite some time. That Tara insisted he abandon his only shield against her was as unnerving as the way his body reacted whenever she was near.

"I never meant to imply that you're childish," he replied in a steady tone.

Far from it! he thought. *If only you knew how hard it's been for me to refrain from acting on the way I see you.*

"It's just that I worry about you, and I don't like feeling that you think I'm incapable of taking care of my own problems."

Since that put matters into a completely different light, one that cast Jonas as a man needing to see himself as strong and capable, Tara held her tongue. Being wise beyond her years, she saw no reason to antagonize him further. Besides, she'd do exactly what she wanted to do, anyway.

Within hours, boxes started arriving. In no time at all they had the makings of a temporary office. Soon the main computer was up and running, paperwork was sorted into piles according to priority, and the temp Tara had hired to run the San Francisco office reported that everything there was going relatively smoothly. Feeling underfoot, Jonas lamented that he was going to have to cancel the upcoming buying trip overseas to which he had been so looking forward.

While much of his business was conducted over the Internet, he still enjoyed periodic forays into dangerous territories. Exposure to infectious diseases and sometimes hostile gunfire were part of the allure. His adventurous lifestyle had served him well during the time he'd been forced to wait in jail for Tara's arrival. As much as he despised his questionable companions, Jonas found them far less formidable than the chieftain of a tribe of headhunters with whom he'd once shared a meal. Of course, the chieftain had been far more honorable than the scumbags who had inhabited the cells next to his.

Tara knew full well that Jonas found the merchandising end of the business rather dull, and she was secretly relieved that he'd been forced to cool his heels for a while. It hadn't escaped her notice that every time she came remotely close to revealing her true feelings to him, he packed up and went abroad. Unable to bring herself to believe it was merely coincidence, she was determined to use this opportunity to force the issue of whether he felt anything more for her than employer-employee respect.

That Jonas did indeed find her incredibly beguiling was not necessarily due to any untoward behavior on her part. He could no more find fault with her decorum than he could her clothes. What she was wearing at the moment was certainly professional. He couldn't exactly blame her for his being so fascinated by the way her skirt hugged her hips and exposed a pair of long silky legs or for the way he covertly studied the swell of her breasts beneath the satiny fabric of her shirt.

It wasn't as if she had deliberately changed the quality or brand of the perfume she wore. Still, her subtle fragrance played havoc with his senses. Every time she came near, it evoked haunting sensual images that could well have landed him in court for sexual harassment had he actually acted on them. Determined that hard work was all he needed to clear his mind and keep him focused, he refused to take a break for the rest of the day.

As evening settled over the sleepy little community like a lacy shawl, Jonas pushed himself away from the computer screen and grumbled that though he was starving, he had no desire to leave the hotel and endure the whispers of "polite society." Happy to accommodate him, Tara reached around him to shut off the computer and call it a day herself. Jonas was enveloped by the flowery scent of her shampoo as her hair brushed his face. The almost imperceptible touch of her hair against his skin produced an incredibly potent flame in the center of his being.

Tara called room service and ordered a bottle of wine and dinner for two. Personally the romantic aspect of it delighted her. The candles, the wine, the fresh flowers all carted in by a young man dressed pristinely in white seemed divinely inspired to help set just the right mood for elegant seduction.

Unfortunately Jonas seemed impervious to the flickering charm of the moment. The food was delicious, and Tara gave little sighs of pleasure with each bite she took. When she asked him to pass her the salt, his hand inadvertently brushed hers, sending shivers all the length of her body.

"Here's to the most wonderful assistant in the world," Jonas said, raising his glass and clinking it gently against hers.

Taking a modest sip, Tara blushed. As potent as

the wine, the compliment warmed her from the inside out.

"I'm glad you know how lucky you are to have me," she replied, batting her eyes exaggeratedly. Since flirting had never been her forte, Tara decided to rely on humor to carry her through any awkward pauses in the conversation.

"I do indeed," Jonas assured her.

Over the years he had come to rely on Tara's strength, common sense and wonderful sense of humor in more than just business matters. She had become his confidante, gently encouraging him to attend the Fortune reunion, then rushing to bail him out of jail without the least hesitation.

With every sip of wine his lovely assistant took, he could see her visibly relax. Remembering the drinking that had so long ago landed her in the slammer with his precocious stepsister, he was sorely tempted to remind her to slow down. Still, she looked so pretty sitting there, all flushed and content, that he hated sounding like her father. She was old enough to have a drink if she wanted one. Thinking how that pink suit complemented her fair coloring, he found himself enjoying the company of such a stunning woman.

The sound of her laughter brushed his dark thoughts away. Deciding it the sexiest sound he'd ever heard, Jonas came to realize more fully just how difficult this forced cohabitation was going to be. It had been hard enough back at the office chasing off thoughts of Tara as anything more than his kid sister's best friend. Here, it would take the fortitude of a saint to ignore that voluptuous body and those mystical dark eyes. How could fate conspire to package innocence and sensuality in such a seductive pink bundle of pure femininity?

Refilling her glass, Jonas told himself that she was safe with him. It wasn't as if she was driving anywhere tonight, thus endangering herself or others. The worst that could happen was that he might have to tuck her into bed. His own drink poised midway in its path from the table to his lips, the thought caught him unawares. By the way his body reacted, he had to pause to wonder who was going to protect her from him.

Ashamed of the direction his thoughts had taken, Jonas sternly reminded himself of all he owed this woman. Certainly more than the kind of one-night sexual gratification that had led to his own birth. He had no intention of ever doing that to another human being. Especially not to such a genuinely sweet thing as Tara.

"I think I'll turn in early," he said, rising from his chair and trying to rouse a yawn. With his body so attuned to the beautiful woman in the room, Jonas seriously doubted he was going to fall asleep anytime soon. The look of disappointment on her face tempted him to sit right back down again. Prudence, however, kept his knees locked in an upright position.

"Good night," Tara murmured. The regret in her voice implied she somehow felt responsible for hastening his departure.

Long after he had retired to his bedroom, Tara sat in the dying candlelight pondering the future. It was apparent that Jonas was bound and determined to be a gentleman. And while she respected his chivalry, she also found it downright infuriating. Unassuming by nature, she was clearly uncomfortable in the role of aggressor. Yet she knew that if she waited for him to make the first move, she would be destined to die an old maid like that preposterous-looking caricature in the deck of cards she remembered playing with as a child.

Contemplating the half-empty bottle of wine, she thought about accidentally stumbling into Jonas's bedroom. She could always blame her misguided sense of direction on the alcohol. As luck would have it, such blatant sexual overtures were not Tara's style. The truth was, she wasn't confident enough about her own sexual prowess to risk throwing herself at him.

Although Jonas wasn't seeing anyone seriously at the moment, she knew he didn't lead a celibate lifestyle. Over time she had watched, with equal measures of envy and disgust, various women blatantly coming on to her boss. Beautiful self-assured women who knew what they wanted and weren't afraid to go after it. Experienced women with no fear that they might prove unsatisfactory in bed.

It was agony for Tara to be so close to the man she loved and yet so far. For all intents and purposes they might as well have been separated by thousands of miles as by a single thin wall. Sighing, Tara pushed herself away from the table. On a whim, she snapped a daisy off the fresh spray on the cart and tucked it behind an ear.

"Tomorrow is another day," she said, melodramatically mimicking one of her favorite fictional characters. Scarlett O'Hara was the kind of woman who would stop at nothing to get her heart's desire. Certain there was a lesson for herself in the character's words, Tara headed off to bed determined to put her troubles behind her for the night.

* * *

After a sound night's sleep, she had a pot of coffee brewing and was ready for work by eight the next morning.

Unlike Tara, her boss was decidedly not a morning person. Yawning widely enough to frighten all flies within range, Jonas straggled into the "office" wearing a pair of button-fly jeans and a tight white T-shirt that defined his muscles all too well. His hair was sticking out in all directions. Tara couldn't decide which impulse was stronger: the one compelling her to run her hands the length of those fabulous biceps or the one urging her to smooth that errant hair. In his disheveled sleepy state, he was enough to make any red-blooded woman's mouth water. Something about those heavy-lidded eyes made her want to abandon work altogether and tuck herself back into bed with him.

"Coffee?" she asked, reining in her fugitive thoughts and slipping into her professional demeanor.

Jonas mumbled something that she could only assume was yes. Setting a fresh cup before him, she looked at him in concern. "Didn't you sleep well?"

He could have killed her. Lifting red-rimmed eyes to meet hers, Jonas glared at her. "Not really," he said, confirming the obvious.

How dare she be so chipper so early in the day? While he'd spent the night tossing and turning, fantasizing about what kind of nightclothes she wore, Tara had apparently been sound asleep, blissfully unaware of his torment. The least she could do was have the decency to be as susceptible as he was to daylight's harsh glare. Indeed, no dark circles, mussed hair or irritability marred the lovely face Tara presented this morning. If anything she looked prettier than ever in a pair of tight jeans and form-fitting sweater. He doubted she was even aware of how every luscious curve of her body was so tauntingly displayed.

Impervious to Jonas's dark mood, Tara offered him a doughnut to "sweeten" him up. He took three. Wondering what it would be like to awake every day to such a bright happy countenance, he couldn't help the smile that tugged at the corners of his mouth. That off-key humming of hers was certainly a nice way to start the day.

A long hot shower and shave helped Jonas feel refreshed. Tara jumped when he stepped back into their office after preparing himself for the day. Hurriedly she got off the phone and asked him if he was feeling any better.

Made suspicious by her guilty blush, Jonas ignored the inquiry. "Who was that?" he wanted to know.

Tara wished she was a better liar. "I was trying to get hold of your uncle," she admitted reluctantly.

The look darkening his features left little doubt that he did not appreciate her meddling.

"I know you've been worried," Tara rushed on, pretending not to notice the way his lips thinned in disapproval. "It sounds like he's going to be all right, after all. Did you know he's scheduled to be released from the hospital any day now?"

"No, I didn't." Jonas's words were as clipped as the heels of marching soldiers. "And aside from how it affects me personally, I don't much care, either."

Even when inwardly panicked, Tara had the amazing ability to look outwardly serene. She decided to remain quiet and let him make the next move. She focused her attention on the correspondence in front of her.

"All right," Jonas growled, hating himself for succumbing to curiosity. "What did he have to say?"

Tara fidgeted with opening a letter to avoid meeting his thunderous expression. "Just that his lawyer had advised him not to speak to you. He sounded pretty weak," Tara added hastily, hoping to douse the fire blazing in Jonas's eyes. "Like he might have been overmedicated."

The last thing she wanted to do was put more strain on an already frayed family bond. Ever the optimist, she was still holding out hope that Jonas could still somehow establish a relationship with his Texas kinsmen. Clearly now, however, was not the time to broach that particularly prickly subject.

"I don't want you to ever speak to that man again. Or any of the Fortunes, for that matter," Jonas said in a tone that left little doubt he expected to be obeyed.

"That could be kind of hard," she responded with a forced determined smile, "considering that it would be hard to swing a cat in this town without hitting one of your relations."

"Then don't go swinging any cats."

Petulance welled up in Tara like a geyser. "How dare you speak to me like I'm fourteen!" she erupted. "I'm a grown woman, and I'll talk to whomever I please, thank you very much. And if you don't stop treating me like a little girl without the good sense God gave a goose, I'm going to swing more than just a cat at you!"

Startled by her fervor, Jonas softened his tone. "All I'm saying is that I would really prefer that you don't

involve yourself with any of my so-called relatives.''
And although he didn't think he owed her any explanation, he offered one, anyway. ''I don't trust them
and I don't want you getting hurt.''

Seeing that the concern clouding those amazing
eyes was for her alone, Tara's indignation melted like
ice cream on a hot summer day. Touched, she willingly sought a compromise.

''I appreciate that you don't want me to get hurt,
Jonas,'' she told him, her own tone softer now, too.
''But you need to realize that *you* are the one in danger here, not me. If somebody is out to frame you for
murder, who knows how far this could go? I can't
stand the thought of someone trying to destroy you.''
Tara's voice cracked with emotion. ''I promise I'll be
careful if you'll do the same.''

Unable to argue with what appeared to be perfectly
sound logic, not to mention moving loyalty, Jonas
decided to take Tara at her word. Unable to do anything about the situation but wait, he turned his attention to the business of the day. It came as no surprise
that his competent assistant had things completely under control. With the exception of some documents
that he needed to sign, Jonas felt more or less in the
way. Furthermore, the news about his uncle had been
unsettling. As much as Jonas hated to admit it, he had
been anxious to be accepted by his new family. It hurt
him deeply that they all suspected him of foul play.
Though relieved to hear that Ryan was to be released
soon, Jonas nonetheless felt insulted that his uncle
refused to so much as speak to him.

How he longed to hop the next plane and put all
this turmoil behind him! Jonas often found himself
hankering for the kind of overseas travel that most

people would find traumatic. He recognized the restlessness he was feeling for what it was—the need to run; to put distance between himself and trouble spelled with a capital Tara.

Unfortunately the law prevented him from following his usual pattern of escape.

The day crawled by. Jonas had difficulty focusing on anything other than the slender curve of his assistant's neck as she bent over her work, the texture of her hair brushing enchantingly against his hand as he reached to take the phone from her, a sweet musky scent that set his pulse throbbing and a guileless pair of eyes framed by lashes so long Jonas thought they should at least warrant a city ordinance. By quitting time, he thought he would go mad if he didn't get out of his incredible shrinking hotel suite.

"I need some air," he announced suddenly.

Startled, Tara pulled her gaze away from the computer screen to study his face. Glancing at her watch, she saved her work with a single keystroke and smiled affably.

"What do you say we go out for dinner?"

Jonas couldn't bring himself to utter the loud "No!" reverberating in his brain. After all, there was no rational reason to decline the invitation, and the last thing he wanted was to hurt Tara's feelings. He just wanted to put some space between them so that he could clear the cobwebs from his head. Hoping that simply getting out of the hotel would be enough to give him some breathing room, Jonas acquiesced to her suggestion. Perhaps she would want to window-shop after dinner and he could make up some excuse to go back to the room and check for mess-

ages. If he didn't get away from her soon, he knew
he was going to have trouble keeping his unruly desire at bay.

Although Tara was aware of how awkward it was
for Jonas to be seen in public, given the charges
against him, she was still excited about going out for
dinner with him. Aside from the fact that she was the
only female in town that he knew, apart from relatives, it was almost like a real date. She ran a brush
through her hair and put on a dab of lipstick for the
occasion. The natural color on her cheeks made the
need for any other makeup unnecessary.

They picked out a small out-of-the-way restaurant
in hopes that no one would recognize Jonas. He directed the hostess to seat them in a dimly lit booth
against the back wall and did his best to ignore the
fact that people craned their necks to stare as they
made their way to their seats. Jonas tried dismissing
their curiosity, knowing that Tara's classic features,
natural elegance and curvaceous figure would have
made her the target of envious gawking even had she
not been seen with Red Rock's most infamous jail-
bird.

For her part, Tara attributed Jonas's restlessness
throughout their meal to the fact that he had virtually
been penned up for too long. All day he had reminded
her of a panther pacing behind the bars of a cage
avariciously eyeing freedom. Growling at anyone
who came too near.

What Tara did not understand was that it was her
own nearness causing his decided unease.

Jonas took pleasure from the fact that Tara so completely enjoyed her meal. Having dated women who

picked daintily at high-priced plates and lied about being full after three mouthfuls, it was refreshing to be with someone with a healthy appetite. Figuring her for the kind of woman who would likely enjoy a good ball game while relishing a hot dog with the works and a plastic cup of frothy beer on the side, Jonas wished he could hop the next plane and whisk her off to Candlestick Park.

It had been a long time since such simple joys had held any appeal for Jonas. As a child he'd had no father to take him to ball games or compete in three-legged races or toss a football around in the backyard. Secretly he had cursed the man who was his real father and made up lame excuses for the stepfather who never once showed up at any of his activities. As a grown man, Jonas tried supplanting hurtful memories by journeying to faraway places and deliberately putting himself in dangerous situations. It had never occurred to him that a simpler answer lay closer at home in a pair of soft brown eyes that had the power to magically make the world seem new all over again.

When Tara finished off the last bite of her chocolate cheesecake with a satisfied sigh, she suggested they catch the early movie showing in town. Thinking it would be a good way to get his mind off work, off his troubles and off a certain pretty blonde, Jonas agreed. He neglected, however, to take into account how his body might react to sitting next to an enchantress in the dark, her fragrance wrapping itself around his senses, effectively blocking out the drama playing on the screen. Tara's laughter was so infectious that he found himself smiling in all the appropriate places even though he wasn't paying a bit of attention to the actors' lines.

Once when something in the film frightened her, Tara grabbed his arm and squeezed hard. He flexed his muscles beneath her hand. No matter how undeserved it might be, her reaction made him feel strong and protective as an overpowering surge of hormones raged through his body. All the while he was wondering why his age wasn't tempering such purely physical reactions with prudence, he enjoyed feeling like her hero.

Clearly this was the epitome of foolishness. And every bit as dangerous for Tara's tender heart as for his jaded one. After all, what could the future hold for a man accused of attempted murder?

Emerging from the darkened theater to a surprisingly soft twilight, Jonas had every intention of separating himself from her for the remainder of the evening on any pretense at all. Why he accepted her suggestion that he accompany her on a walk through the park before turning in for the day was as much a mystery to him as who had tried to poison Uncle Ryan Fortune. August days tend to be punishing in Texas, and this one had been no exception. The cooler temperature of the falling night was a welcome relief as they strolled up to a Civil War cannon that seemed horribly out-of-place next to modern-day playground equipment.

The park was deserted save for one lone family. The parents were loading up the remnants of their picnic, folding tablecloths and blankets and gathering their protesting brood. The father chased his youngest, a red-haired little girl who squealed in delight at what she perceived as a game of tag. Tara and Jonas kept their gazes away from one another, as if being alone could somehow make disturbing longings for such a simple loving lifestyle disappear like the light fading from the sky.

Uncomfortable with the direction her thoughts were taking, Tara challenged Jonas to race her to the swings. When he staunchly refused, she called him an old fuddy-duddy and set off on her own. She looked so beautiful with her thick mane of golden hair streaming out behind her that Jonas couldn't help but be stirred by the sight. He took off after her and, despite her sizable head start, beat her to the swings.

How good it felt to abandon the heavy mantle of responsibility his stepfather had forced on him all those years ago. Though Jonas declared himself too mature to climb aboard a swing himself, he positioned himself behind Tara and pushed her, gently at first and then, at her urging, more energetically. Giggling, she arched her back and pointed her toes toward the heavens. It was one of the most innocently erotic sights Jonas had ever beheld.

Tara felt the breath freeze in her lungs each time he sent her in the direction of the stars. Exhaling into the clouds above, she reveled in her earthbound freedom. Despite the dreadful circumstances of the charges that had brought her here, she felt incredibly happy. For some time she had been trying to get Jonas to notice her as a woman. Tonight she felt certain she was accomplishing her goal, not with mascara and form-fitting clothes and expensive perfume, but with the kind of genuine dialogue that truly connects one heart to another.

With each pass of the swing, they took turns disclosing bits and pieces of their personal lives. For example, Jonas discovered that Tara was allergic to pistachios, that she hated horror movies, that she adored Shakespeare's sonnets and that her loyalty to her father sprung not out of a sense of obligation but out of a heart that seemed too sweet and good to be true.

Tara learned that, as a boy, Jonas had wanted to be a cowboy, that he despised broccoli and that his hero had been Han Solo from the *Star Wars* series. He also painfully recalled for her how his stepfather used to make him beg for enough spare change to buy a soda with the rest of the guys after the baseball games where he shone as a talented athlete. Not that anyone in his family ever made it to his games, he added bitterly. Soon thereafter, Jonas got a newspaper route, vowing never to have to beg anyone for anything ever again.

Certainly not for love.

Though Jonas did not put it into words, it was obvious that he felt begging for love was a waste of time and energy because deep down he believed himself unlovable. If his own father hadn't cared enough to stick around and see how he turned out, let alone make an occasional token child-support payment, how could he expect someone as devoted to the ideals of family as Tara to put her faith in him? Having brought his own mother nothing but emotional ill-treatment for the sacrifices she had made on his behalf, he could never ask another woman to endure similar heartache in the fickle name of love.

As a teenager, Tara had been privy to glimpses of Jonas's troubled childhood only through her association with his stepsister, Ellen, who refused to have any of her friends over to her house because of her father's bad temper. Thus the bitterness with which Jonas spoke of his stepfather came as no surprise to her. The fact that he had come to Texas at all for the Lost Heirs Reunion was clearly indicative of his subconscious desire to connect with the birth father who had abandoned him—even if he was dead. It was a shame that Jonas's experience in Red Rock only served to bolster his belief that it wasn't worth the time or effort to cultivate family ties. He openly vowed that he would never allow himself to feel so vulnerable again.

Tara argued against his logic, claiming that love was the only thing in this world for which she was willing to risk everything.

"All I really want out of this life," she declared beneath the faint glimmer of stars poking through the darkening sky, "is a love like my parents had. When my mother died, Dad vowed never to marry again. It was even worse than when we found out he had a rare blood disease. Worse because it's been far harder for him to live without Mom than it has been for him to deal with his condition."

The longing in Tara's voice for the kind of love her parents had shared almost made Jonas wish he believed in such nonsense as love at first sight, happy endings and lifetime commitments. He was glad to hear that she was considering hiring a nurse to stay with her father so that she wouldn't have to move back into the old brownstone where she and her two older brothers had grown up.

"That's good," Jonas said, correctly reading the worry in her voice when she spoke of her father's health. "Someone as lovely and vibrant as you shouldn't live life for an ailing parent."

"I'm all he has left," she said simply.

"What about your brothers?" Jonas asked pointedly. Unable to ignore the fact that her hair glinted with gold highlights as the breeze rustled through its soft tendrils, he found himself unaccountably angry with her siblings. "Don't they feel the same obligation you do?"

"They're married and have lives of their own to lead."

Jonas felt a rush of indignation sweep through him. "Why should your life be any less meaningful just because you happen to be single and the youngest in the family? How did you come to be designated as the responsible party in the family?"

Brushing aside the question like a swarm of pesky mosquitoes, she joked, "Dad says he's waiting for me to get married before he kicks the bucket."

Thinking to himself that old men shouldn't make unfair demands on their children, Jonas dragged her swing to a halt and twisted the chains around so that she faced him. As much as this evening seemed like a gift handed to him straight from the missing pages of his childhood, he didn't want Tara to misunderstand his intentions. Knowing how much she looked up to him, he didn't want to lead her on. Old painful memories flooded his senses and cracked his heart open as he attempted to explain the reason he so desperately needed to keep his emotional distance.

"Personally I don't put much faith in the institution of marriage. When my mother discovered she was pregnant with me, her own family cast her aside as a cheap tramp rather than a confused young girl who had made a mistake. In an attempt to correct that mistake, she compounded it, instead, by enslaving herself to Nicolas Goodfellow just to give me a name. Let me assure you, marriage certainly didn't make my stepfather any less cruel a man. Nor did it keep my alleged birth father out of other women's beds. Newspaper stories at the time indicated that he was with his twenty-two-year-old assistant at the time of his death. Regardless of what Ryan Fortune says, I doubt his brother ever gave a thought to any of the children he'd sired outside his marriage—maybe not even those recognized by law.''

''You don't know that,'' Tara refuted softly. Hearing the anguish in his voice, she wanted him to know that not all marriages were as disastrous as the ones to which he referred and that just because Cameron Fortune was flawed did not automatically cast all his relatives in the same mold. ''The fact that your uncle went out of his way to locate you after all these years says something for your roots, doesn't it?''

''Only that I'd like to pull them up and stomp on them.''

Tara recognized the lie as a way to protect Jonas's wounded heart. She understood being truly rooted as a crucial need of the human soul. She knew that Jonas had come to Texas seeking the kind of family that she herself had taken for granted in her own life only to become embroiled in a plot of greed and deceit.

''Men like me aren't cut out for family life,'' Jonas told her. ''I get my kicks out of poking my finger in the eye of old established businessmen like my stepfather who said I could never best their efforts. Marriage to a job is more than fulfilling to a nomad like myself who finds his pleasures in faraway places.''

Four

"I wouldn't be so sure about that," Tara said, lifting her feet off the ground and giving Jonas an enigmatic smile.

Around and around she spun, her hair whipping out behind her in a yellow arc as she twirled joyfully beneath the Milky Way.

"There are so many stars up there to wish upon," she said. "Why don't you let someone who hasn't forgotten how to dream help you pick out a special one to wish upon tonight?"

"Hey, you kids! Don't you know there's a curfew in this town?"

The sound of authority blasting over the police-car speaker system caused Jonas to jump away from the swings and into his past. He hadn't felt so foolish since he'd been caught making out in his rebuilt little Mustang way back in his senior year of high school.

He had been so engrossed in conversation with Tara that all concept of time had escaped him. Stepping out of the darkness, he advanced upon the police car.

A glance at Jonas's solid physique assured the officer on duty that this was no kid. The deep sure sound of his voice also put the young cop at ease. Relieved it wasn't his shirttail relative Sheriff Grayhawk peering through the shadows at him, Jonas wished the officer a good-night and accepted his apology for accosting them in such a brusque manner.

The sound of Tara's laughter at the officer's mistake made him somehow feel younger than he had in years. That he was only thirty-four didn't negate the fact that he'd been old since his childhood when fate had thrust an adult's responsibilities onto his thin shoulders. When other teenagers had been out on dates, Jonas had been working long hours doing his stepfather's bidding. It struck him as ironic that it took criminal charges to slow him down long enough to enjoy a movie and an evening stroll.

As they ambled along the street and crossed over to the hotel, Jonas impulsively took Tara's hand. He didn't want his actions to be construed as anything more than friendship. Indeed, the feeling of being connected to another human being in such a natural way was special. More special, actually, than the sexual dalliances that so often left him feeling hollow and somehow used. Jonas studied the white picket fences delineating one house from another along the pleasant tree-lined street. Life seemed so sheltered here, so picture-perfect that for a moment he almost forgot there was an attempted-murder charge hanging over his head. Almost.

Tara's suggestion that they pass the remainder of

the evening playing cards back in their suite sounded
as refreshing as the lemonade they had shared at the
movie. Maintaining that she was the all-time hearts
champion of the world, she challenged Jonas to a
match. Having few occasions to engage in such activities when he was growing up, it seemed strange
to Jonas how much fun a simple game could be. He
suspected it had more to do with the way his opponent
played with such gusto, as if her salary was riding on
every hand, than with any determination on his part
to keep the mood light.

"Good thing we're not playing strip poker," he
grumbled, trying to dismiss the erotic image that
statement evoked. "I doubt you'd have the decency
to leave a man a pair of socks."

Tara grinned as he threw in his hand. Although not
even one chaste kiss had elevated the evening beyond
anything platonic, she couldn't remember when she'd
had such a good time. Convinced that the strongest
relationships were initially based on friendship, she
held out hope that Jonas could not continue to resist
her charms indefinitely.

Had she been more experienced in such matters,
Tara might have realized that he had shared more of
himself with her tonight than he had with any other
woman. She might have seen the desire smoldering
in his eyes when he said simply, "Good night, then,"
with a trace of gravel in his voice.

"Sweet dreams," she replied softly at the sound of
his bedroom door closing behind him.

She lay awake a long time in her bed wondering if
the pounding of her heart wouldn't somehow keep
Jonas from sleeping. The cadence it was beating out
was far wilder than the jungle drums of which he was

so fond. After a long internal battle over whether she shouldn't have simply asked him for a good-night kiss, she at last fell into a fitful sleep during which she dreamed she was cornered by a ferocious tiger. It growled as she reached out her hand to it. Tara sensed that if she could but pet it, it would shrink to the size of a house cat. Instead, it snapped its massive jaws together around her arm.

Tara awoke with a start, clutching her arm. Disoriented, she had difficulty placing herself. Remembering at last that she was in a strange bed in a faraway state imagining noises in the middle of the night, she finally located the clock by her bed. Its neon numbers glowed 2:15 a.m. Still unnerved by the thought of being eaten alive in her dreams, it occurred to her that she wasn't simply imagining those strange sounds in the other room.

It occurred to her that someone might have broken in and was trying to harm Jonas. Ryan Fortune was a very influential man in Red Rock. It only stood to reason that there were those angry enough at the man accused of hurting Ryan who just might try to do Jonas in. Those willing to seek their own style of retribution.

As silently as the big cat she had been dreaming about, Tara slipped from beneath the covers and grabbed the nearest weapon available: a brass lamp just the right weight and size for clunking an intruder over the head. Adrenaline surged through her blood and heightened her resolve. Thus armed, she crept into the living room ready to do battle. Directed by a soft dull light, she raised the heavy lamp over her head with the intention of bringing it down with all her might.

Sitting there in the chair dazedly watching late-night television was Jonas.

Bleary-eyed, he looked up from the silvery light of the screen and gazed at her in confusion. Wearing nothing but a robe, he had been channel surfing, vainly trying to quell the beast within him that would allow him no rest.

"I...I heard something," Tara stammered, sinking into an armchair across from him. Pale and shaking, she clutched the polished base of the lamp to her breast.

"What are you doing with that?" he asked, pointing to her weapon of choice.

"Protecting you," she admitted with a shaky little smile that didn't come anywhere near her eyes.

Jonas snorted. The thought of this woman risking her life to save him would have been laughable had it not been so incredibly brave.

"Has it ever occurred to you that you might be the one in need of protection?" he asked softly.

Tara shook her head, her eyes seeking his through the dim haze of the television's glare.

"Sweetheart, what am I going to do with you?" he asked in a voice laced with uncertain desire.

Tara had a good idea, but seeing as she'd already made a fool of herself, she hesitated to offer it. Right now it was hard focusing on anything other than the speculation that Jonas was wearing nothing beneath that robe but his own sweet skin. She had always suspected that he was not a pajama man, and it would be a thrill to discover whether she was right.

Taking in the plunging neckline of her baby-doll pajamas, Jonas made a wry observation. "I see you came dressed to kill."

A hot blush crept up her neck in an all-too-visible path. Chastely crossing her arms over her chest, she explained, "There wasn't exactly time to grab a robe."

"No need to apologize. If anyone should be sorry, it's me for waking you up and scaring you." Gesturing toward the television with the remote control, Jonas muted the sound. "Just because I can't sleep doesn't give me the right to deprive you of yours."

Tara jumped to an obvious assumption about the cause of his insomnia. "I know you're worried about the investigation, but I have every faith in the system that the charges will be dropped. They can't convict an innocent man. They just can't—"

The sound that stuck in Jonas's throat was half chortle, half moan. "That isn't what's causing my insomnia."

"It isn't?"

"No. It's you, Tara. You've been tormenting me, haunting my dreams day and night."

Tara's pulse quickened, throbbing noticeably in the hollow of her throat. Considering how long she'd been waiting to hear those words, she was unaccountably nervous. No matter how many times she'd played this scene in her head, she still wasn't prepared for the predatory look that devoured her from head to toe.

Reading the uncertainty in her expression, Jonas offered her a gentlemanly out. "There's still time to run. I won't try to stop you if you decide to go, but if that's what you want, you need to go now."

"But I don't want to go," she whispered over the hammering of a heart too foolish to recognize it was in danger.

Succumbing to a passion that was beyond his control, his understanding, Jonas held out his arms to this woman he'd tried so valiantly to resist. It was important that she come to him on her own accord. He did not want to feel that he was forcing himself on her in any way whatsoever.

Abandoning the lamp on the floor, Tara rose to her feet. On knees that felt gelatinous, she took a step toward the dream that had been eluding her for so long. Entering the circle of Jonas's strong embrace, she wrapped her arms around the solid column of his neck and slipped onto his lap. His arousal was pronounced through the robe. Tara gasped. It was a heady feeling to know she had such an effect on him. She opened his robe and ran her hands across the expanse of his wide chest. Dark tufts of hair felt silken beneath fingertips shaking with anticipation. His skin was so hot that she hoped he wasn't running a fever.

Sliding his hands beneath her short gown, Jonas discovered that Tara, too, was on fire. That slinky material was no softer to the touch than flesh that was firm and warm and inviting. With all the determination of Pandora opening that fateful box, Jonas drew her near for a kiss. He could not remember such sweet lips touching his. Running his tongue along the inner seam of those honeyed lips, he found that she tasted like sunshine and sugar and unsullied dreams. When she moaned, he deepened the kiss, seeking the hidden pleasures of her mouth and ravaging her very soul.

Tara sighed her surrender, marking the capitulation to a dream too long deferred. The wait had not lessened any imagined gratification, rather only intensified the longing of a heart overflowing with emotion.

She nibbled on Jonas's full lower lip as if fearing that if she let this kiss end, it might be the last they ever shared. But Jonas had no intention of stopping now. He couldn't have even if he'd wanted to. Astonished at the pleasure he gave, Tara tossed her head back, reveling in the feeling of his lips traversing a path from her earlobe to the sensitive hollow at the base of her throat.

Kittenish noises came from somewhere deep inside her. Taking Jonas's hands into her own, she smothered them with kisses. She had always had a secret fetish for those big masterful hands. She was delighted to discover how gentle they were when he used them to cup her breasts and explore their sensitive tips with the pad of each thumb.

So enthralled was she in that glorious sensation that she was almost unaware of Jonas pulling her gown over her head. In the glow of the muted television screen, he gazed upon her nakedness with unabashed admiration. Like a man who had gone without water for too long, he desperately longed to slake his thirst.

"You really don't know how incredibly beautiful you are, do you," he said in disbelief.

Embers long banked in those smoky eyes burst into flame. With the reverence of someone entering sacred ground, he bent his head to suckle at one ripe breast.

Tara felt a tingling that started in her stomach and radiated throughout her entire body. Calling out his name as if in prayer, she cradled his head at her bosom, ruffling his soft dark hair between splayed fingers. The next thing she knew she was being lifted into his strong arms and carried into his bedroom. Her nightclothes lay forgotten upon the floor beside the lamp and his robe.

Jonas laid his precious cargo on the bed and stood a long while above her, admiring her splendor. Only the light glowing in her eyes could compete with the halo of her hair spilling in golden waves on her pillow. Brimming with unshed tears of joy, Tara beckoned him to join her in bed.

"I want this to be good for you," Jonas whispered, lowering himself over her. "I want to go slow. I'll do my best to make it last as long as I can."

His body, however, was having trouble obeying his brain's commands. Tara opened herself to him like an exotic flower slowly unfolding beneath the gentle rays of the sun. Unable to wait a second longer, Jonas slipped inside her, groaning in pleasure at the incredible fit of their bodies. By the time he could register that tight resistance met and broken with a single stroke, it was too late to turn back.

He moaned.

She was a virgin. Having suspected it all along, Jonas remonstrated himself for being such a brute. For not being better able to restrain himself. Assuming the tears falling down her cheeks had arisen from pain he had inflicted, he kissed them tenderly away.

"I never meant to hurt you," he whispered.

Tara willed him to understand that her tears sprang not from pain but from the discovery that sharing her body and soul with the man she loved was more infinitely beautiful than she had ever imagined. She had only dreamed that it could be like this between a woman and a man, that souls could join in such a joyous physical manner.

"The only way you'll hurt me is to stop loving me," she admitted with something that sounded more like a gasp than a sob.

Bringing her to exquisite joy was more gratifying than Jonas could ever put into words. Understanding that her newfound sexuality was as yet rather shy, he was as gentle as could be, leading her carefully to the top of a high mountain cloaked in sensual mystery. He took care to make sure she experienced every erotic shudder that rocked through her body before at last tumbling over the edge of that precipice with her. Crying out in ecstasy, they clung to one another, trusting that angels would carry them safely back to earth.

In the aftermath of their lovemaking, Jonas looked tenderly at the woman in his arms. That she had offered him her virginity was a gift more precious than any he had ever received.

Jonas cursed himself for not bothering to use any kind of protection. That they had been too caught up in their passion at the time to give it any thought was not much of an excuse. As far as he was concerned, Tara was completely blameless in the matter. He was the one who should know better. If by some statistical improbability this one incident resulted in pregnancy, Jonas would do right by the baby—unlike his own father who had shown no more compunction about leaving him and his mother behind than one might abandon a litter of mongrel pups.

Overcome with guilt, he vowed to never let such an oversight happen again.

The way she was looking at him with those soft trusting eyes, as if he was some kind of hero, instead of an insensitive beast who had just satisfied his physical needs and stripped her of all innocence, made him feel like the world's biggest heel.

When he started to speak, Tara put a finger to his

lips. "If you dare apologize to me, I'll cry for real," she threatened.

Thus chastised, Jonas agreed not to seek pardon, but rather to enjoy the special time they had together. Kissing her forehead and eyelids, the tip of her nose and the dimples on either side of her mouth, he encouraged her to explore her own sexual needs and desires.

Surprised by his stamina and insatiable desire, Tara tentatively proceeded to indulge her newfound sexuality. Although a late bloomer, she was an apt pupil, who instinctively knew how to give, as well as how to receive, pleasure. If their initial lovemaking was like going over Niagara Falls without so much as a barrel, what followed was a gentle exploration on a lazy winding river through foreign territory.

Languid, uninhibited and thorough.

Spent at last, Jonas gathered Tara close to his heart with the unspoken promise that he would cherish the memory of this moment forever.

Five

For the first time since Jonas had hired her, Tara slept in on a workday. Waking in her lover's arms was such a delicious feeling that she wanted to cling to it for as long as she possibly could. The familiar musky fragrance of their bodies flushed with heat and entangled in the sheets was definitely something she wanted to cherish. She pressed every detail like rose petals in her memory book. Safe, warm and secure, she resisted the very thought of getting out of bed.

Jonas's eyes were gentle on her as he tucked an errant strand of hair behind her ear. "Good morning, sleepyhead," he said, kissing her still-puffy lips.

"Morning," she mumbled, half-asleep. "If I'm asleep, please don't pinch me."

A loud knock at the front door was just as effective at bringing her to full consciousness. *Don't answer that!* she wanted to cry, hoping that by ignoring the summons they could somehow keep the world from their door indefinitely. But it was already too late. Jonas bounded from the bed, searching for his robe on the floor in the other room.

Tara noticed he left without so much as a backward glance in her direction. Sinking deeper into her pillow, she wondered at the transformation that had taken place overnight to change him into such a ray of morning sunshine. It usually took at least two cups of strong coffee to get him started. When he returned a moment later carrying a huge tray of croissants, fresh fruit and steaming cappuccino, Tara couldn't have been more surprised had he walked in with the president himself. The delicious aroma alone was enough to make a person gain five pounds.

"Breakfast in bed!" she exclaimed. Unaccustomed to such royal treatment, she was clearly delighted.

Jonas was pleased by her reaction. That smile lighting that pretty face made opening the curtains unnecessary. How refreshing to be with someone who could be so easily made happy. Most of the women he knew worked hard at appearing unimpressed with diamonds, furs and penthouses.

"My lady," he said with an affected accent that lent itself to the moment.

Sitting up, Tara propped a pillow behind her back and invitingly patted the vacant space beside her in the bed. Taking his cue, Jonas passed her the tray before dropping his robe to the floor and sliding back beneath the still-warm covers. The meal was almost as sumptuous as the banquet they made of one another. Between nibbles they managed to taste most of the food on the tray.

Happily resigned to spending the entire glorious

day in bed, Tara trailed a strawberry along Jonas's broad naked chest before bringing it to his lips. She didn't think she would ever be able to get enough of this man. Becoming part of him was the best thing that had ever happened to her. Nervous that he might expect some kind of wild gymnastic performance from her in bed, she was relieved to discover that he was more than content to indulge in long lavish explorations of each other's bodies. Such glorious intimacy was the stuff of girlish fantasies in which secret wishes were shared with nothing more than a look. Never had Tara dreamed such wishes could actually come true.

It had taken a certain measure of courage to offer herself to this man so completely. Body and soul. But the rewards of doing so were beyond words. Trapped for so long by her own insecurities, Tara wanted to throw open the window and declare her love to the entire world. Happiness welled up inside her like a spring overflowing its banks. Scolding herself for ever doubting the magic of love, she wanted Jonas to know how utterly committed to him she was. Sighing, she traced the outline of his heart on his chest.

"I love you," she whispered, feeling its beat skip erratically beneath her fingertips.

The sound of those three little words echoed in the dark caverns of Jonas's conscience. How he wished she could take them back. He could not repeat them to Tara without being a hypocrite. Admittedly the sex had been great. Better than great, actually. Fantastic. The best he'd ever experienced, to be completely honest. Still, a heart as wary as his understood that didn't necessarily translate into love. Too many women had uttered that same proclamation to him in hopes of binding him to them. Refusing to make a mockery of his feelings, he typically responded by offering them objects less costly than his heart. Things like money and prestige and lovemaking techniques that took into consideration a woman's special needs.

Jonas suspected that would only insult a true lady like Tara. He didn't know how to be honest with her without being cruel. When she looked at him with those gentle brown eyes all misted over with emotion, how could he possibly explain to her that love was for suckers? Love made young women like Tara hostages to ailing old men like her father. It bound his own mother to a bitter man and sapped the life from her body as surely as a disease.

Only a free man had a right to promise a woman his heart. Long ago Jonas promised himself never to be anything like his father, a man who built false hopes and took the broken pieces of a woman's heart as a souvenir of their shared passion.

Rolling onto her side, Tara looked into Jonas's eyes. Sighing, she took his face into her hand and confided with the kind of typical candor that rocked Jonas's whole world, "Are you aware that nothing would make me happier than to have your children? How many would you like? A dozen maybe?"

"A dozen?" he croaked, almost choking on the word.

The thought of fathering one child was enough to send him into a tailspin. Possibilities swirled in his head in dark vivid colors.

"Tara," he said softly, "we need to talk."

Eager to assure him that she would be there for him for the rest of their lives, she sat up in bed attentively.

"I want to apologize for failing to use any protection. It was wrong of me to put you in such a position, and I promise it won't happen again. I have no intention of fathering a child out of wedlock. Rest assured that if anything should happen, I'll be there for you."

"You're going to make a wonderful daddy someday," Tara assured him.

Knowing instinctively that Jonas would come to love any child they begat as deeply as she, she fought back the tears that threatened to give away just how much she wanted to start a family with him.

Last night he had allowed her a glimpse of his soul. In the bright light of the rising sun, Tara hoped to be granted full disclosure. She longed to reassure him that there was nothing about him that she found in the least distasteful and that he was a man who had very special gifts to offer a wife and children.

Secretly startled by her assessment, Jonas responded with a vehement shake of his head. Doubt clouded his sky-blue eyes. How could he let her down easily without completely devastating her?

Idiot! This was the very reason he had tried so desperately to avoid tumbling into bed with her. Jonas knew she would read more into sex than he did.

"Your first time is always emotional," he said, sounding more clinically detached than he meant to.

Tara laughed at his somber tone. She wasn't going to let him off the hook with any modern-day psychobabble on sexual relationships. Reading not from a book on the subject but from her heart, she proclaimed, "I would hope that every time is emotional."

Unable to keep the regret and the guilt from his voice, he told her, "You deserve better than me."

"There is no better," came her swift reply.

Her earnestness made him feel guilty and trapped. There had to be a way of explaining to this earthbound angel that she shouldn't tether herself to someone as grounded by resentments as he. Having already confided that she wanted children, how could he disclose that he wanted none? Ever. Or that, soured on the institution of marriage, he intended to end his days as a devout bachelor?

Had she not been a virgin the night before, had she not been his friend, had she not murmured those poisonous words *I love you,* they might still have been able to forge a mutually advantageous relationship. As it stood, those words erected a barrier that Jonas didn't think he could ever surmount.

What he felt for Tara was strong, but he had no intention of labeling it love. Lust maybe. And while that might be enough for him, he knew it was wrong to keep a doe-eyed woman tied to him waiting for a proposal that was never coming. However astonishing the sex between them might be, it was just not fair to ask a young woman with hopes of starting a family to settle for being his mistress. Yet the mere idea of her in another man's bed left the metallic taste of jealousy in his mouth.

Tara's eyes reminded Jonas of brown satin as she assured him gently, "If you'll just tell me what's on your mind, I promise I'll listen and not judge."

It was a tempting offer. All his life Jonas had struggled to make himself heard. His mother had been so concerned about appeasing the monster of a man she had married that she had constantly shushed the child tugging at her dress. The stepfather who resented him for his bloodline had neither the time nor the inclination to listen to anything a bastard child had to say. The many women who had frequented Jonas's bed cared more about his status and outward appearance than they did about his feelings. Even the lost family that claimed they wanted him back in their midst held him responsible for a heinous crime without ever bothering to listen to his side of the story.

What was it about Tara's gentle demeanor that made Jonas want to take a chance on her actually listening to and perhaps even understanding him? He supposed there was always the possibility that she might truly love him for who he really was—not some hero she'd embellished in her mind over the years they had shared office space. Kissing her softly on the lips, he was just on the verge of unburdening his heart when the telephone rang.

With mixed feelings of regret and relief, Jonas took the call. His clipped responses to the caller gave little clue as to the nature of their conversation, but the way he snapped the receiver back in its cradle was indication enough that Jonas was unsettled by what had passed between them.

A vision of mussed loveliness, Tara looked at him expectantly. With her hair spilling around her shoulders in a golden shimmer, she reminded him of Sleeping Beauty. Unfortunately this princess was awakening to the hard realities of life rather than the blissful kind of happily-ever-after that make fairy tales so enduring.

"That was Sheriff Grayhawk telling me to come down to the station," he explained, running a hand through his shock of dark hair.

"What's the matter?" she asked, instantly alert.

"Apparently I've been cleared of the charges and I'm free to go."

Throwing her arms around his neck, Tara whooped in delight and demanded details. Jonas quickly explained how the bottle of port wine that he had brought to the reunion, the one he had demanded be tested, was found not to have any traces of poison in it. Therefore the police had to conclude that the culprit had slipped poison into the decanter into which Ryan Fortune had poured the wine. And from which he had unwittingly been taking a daily dose of laced port until the day he had been rushed to the hospital. This latest discovery narrowed down the suspects by one. Jonas was free to go with sincere apologies from Sheriff Grayhawk, whom he suspected was dreading having to face his wife with the news that her uncle's attempted murderer was still on the loose.

And was likely one of the family.

Tara was concerned only with the news that Jonas was a free man. Free to concentrate on their relationship now without any more worries about going to prison as an innocent man.

"I have an idea of how we could celebrate," she said in a silken voice that belied the extent of her sexual experience.

Quirking an eyebrow at her, Jonas inquired what exactly she had in mind. What she whispered into his ear had him reaching over to the nightstand for his billfold. He withdrew a condom and had it quickly in place before she proceeded to show him without words just what her idea of a real celebration was all about. It involved every inch of his body: arms, legs, fingertips, tongues and the sensitive spots that lovers linger over. Tara did not hold back, giving freely of her love. Refusing to be shackled by her doubts—or his.

The sight of his big masculine hand caressing the length of her body made Tara sigh contentedly. An eternity of lovemaking stretched before them like a sandy beach kissed by the sun. Taking her bare breasts in both hands, Jonas ran his thumbs over their hardened peaks. Her body was warm and soft and inviting as she opened her mouth to his probing tongue. An instant later Jonas was on top of her, coaxing submissive little sounds from somewhere deep in her throat. Desire flared at the touch of bare skin against bare skin, licking at the inside of Tara's thighs, which he skillfully nudged apart with a knee.

"My love," she murmured, taking hold of him by the shaft and directing him into her waiting slickness.

Burning with a feverish need to consume her, Jonas filled her with himself. Tilting her hips upward, Tara urged him to lose control and bury himself in her willing flesh. Urged him to take her with him over the edge and back again on a journey of excruciatingly exquisite pleasure. She was intimately aware of the beauty of their bodies joined. His all hard planes and muscles. Hers soft curves. Riding the swell of passion, they made love wildly. Gently. Passionately. As if they had never touched each other before. As if they knew each other as lovers from a past lifetime.

Shuddering in his arms, Tara offered herself to him wholly, holding tight to the hope that Jonas would eventually relinquish his dark secrets and allow the hurt inside him to be healed by the balm of her sweet love.

After the way Ryan Fortune had so rudely dismissed Tara when she had tried contacting him, it gave Jonas great satisfaction to snub him in a similar fashion the following day. With her hand over the receiver, Tara implored him to accept the phone call from his uncle, who had been released from the hospital and was apparently recuperating nicely. She understood only too well how deeply the Fortunes' suspicions had hurt Jonas. She also knew that forgiveness was the key to unlocking his aching heart. As long as Jonas insisted on holding on to the bitter feelings of the dispossessed, she feared he would never be truly capable of trusting another person not to abandon him. Of accepting unconditional love.

Or of giving it.

"I'm sorry," Tara lied. "But Mr. Goodfellow is already on his way to the airport.

It wasn't much of a lie. For all intents and purposes, Jonas had one foot in the air already. There was a long pause as Tara listened to what Ryan Fortune had to say. By the time he finished, she sounded far less emotionally removed than a mere secretary would be inclined to be.

"I'll give him the message," she promised before hanging up.

Looking oddly pale and shaky, she valiantly tried to do just that.

Jonas, however, assured her that he wanted no part of his uncle's apology.

She broke into his angry diatribe about the Fortunes to ask in a hushed and hurt tone of voice, "Why didn't you tell me?"

"Tell you what?"

"That as part of the Fortune family, you're to receive a substantial sum of money?"

Jonas laughed as if she had said something funny. "How much money does it take to buy off a forgotten child? To shush a bastard son who might run to the tabloids and give the high-and-mighty Fortunes a very public black eye?"

His eyes turned the color of ominous storm clouds. "Why does it matter to you, anyway?"

"Only so much as it affects our relationship," she said honestly. "Surely you know I don't want you for your money."

"And I don't need the Fortunes for their money," he asserted. "Even though Auntie Miranda casually mentioned an amount at our little family get-together, I dare say that was before good old Uncle Ryan was poisoned. Before everyone jumped to the conclusion that I was a murderer."

"Ryan maintains the offer is still good," Tara informed him.

For the life of her, she couldn't figure out why Jonas was so angry at the thought of receiving money from the Fortunes—unless he was afraid that the offer was a means of controlling him, as his stepfather had tried doing.

"Let me assure you that phony promises issued via the good fairy can't buy me. Nothing can," Jonas said with a conviction born of pain and the knowledge that self-made men like him were beholden to no one.

Tara understood there was more to this issue than money alone. "You have to realize that we're talking about family here. It's hardly fair to hold it against your uncle that he was poisoned—"

"Family!" he guffawed. "A family of philanderers and murderers that any man could be proud of. Don't forget, Tara, whoever did try to kill Ryan is still on the loose and more than likely one of the family members present on the night of the reunion.''

He refused to hear another word from her on the subject. Offered his freedom from Red Rock, he didn't hesitate to take it. He wasn't about to allow anyone, no matter how sweet and tempting, to manipulate him into staying another minute in this crummy little town. Since the place was too small to boast an airport, he asked Tara to book him on the next flight back to San Francisco out of San Antonio.

Hurt that he expected her to stay behind and tie up loose ends for him, she nonetheless put on a bright smile. As much as she wanted to join him, she accepted his edict as part of her job. She tried to rationalize away her hurt feelings with the thought that she should probably just be happy that it was too late to reschedule that European buying trip.

For a relatively short distance, the drive to San Antonio was one of the longest trips Tara had ever taken. Jonas was unusually quiet. Assuming he was attempting to come to grips with the possibility that the Fortunes' offer was genuine, Tara contemplated the irony of his situation. The father who never even knew of his existence had left him a fortune in more than that name alone. Glancing at her companion's pensive expression, Tara wondered if he wasn't, in fact, trying to figure out a way to let her down gently.

Doubts about losing her virginity to a man who had no intention of ever marrying her began playing in her head to the tune of her mother's warnings. *Why buy the cow when the milk's free?* Rebecca Summers had asked with a knowing shake of her head. In her mother's world, a woman's desirability was inexorably linked to playing hard to get and remaining virtuous up until one's wedding night.

Saying that he didn't want Tara going to any trouble, Jonas suggested that she simply drop him off at the airport entrance. Of course, she wouldn't hear of it. She accompanied him to his terminal. They barely had time to check his bags through and validate his ticket before seating for his flight was called.

"I'll see you in a couple of days," Tara assured him through a smile that felt too tight for her teeth.

For a second she didn't think he was even going to kiss her goodbye. Her heart swelled with pain. His eagerness to leave her behind was beginning to feel an awful lot like a brush-off.

"Goodbye," Jonas said, really looking at her for what seemed the first time since leaving Red Rock.

His eyes softened. Sweeping aside the overwhelming urge to rush onto that plane and get his life back to normal, he took her face gently in his hands and bent down to kiss her goodbye. Soft and inviting, her lips quivered beneath his. Tasting her sweetness one more time was nothing short of soul-shattering. Time slowed, and it seemed that all the images outside the periphery of their embrace simply faded into fuzziness.

It felt as if he was trying to permanently imprint in her brain his claim to her heart. As if Tara was likely to forget it.

Her eyelids closed in bliss, her knees melted and her worries dissolved as the world spun madly about her. It took her a moment to realize that the kiss had ended. And yet another to regain any semblance of composure. Without another word, Jonas turned and boarded his plane.

Squaring her shoulders, Tara headed back to Red

Rock. The open plains of Texas lend themselves well to contemplation.

She suspected that there would always be a part of Jonas that would belong to no one until he finally came to grips with his past. Certainly money alone could not buy him love or make up for a childhood plagued by guilt and emotional abuse.

And as long as she had to remain in Red Rock, she might as well maximize her time there. Dismissing Jonas's warning that he didn't want her interfering in his personal life, she considered how best to pick up the pieces of his shattered legacy. It didn't matter how hopeless it appeared, she knew she had to try.

Their future was riding on it.

Six

Ever efficient, Tara had their temporary office packed up in just a day and a half. Or approximately forever, according to her heart's calculations, since Jonas hadn't called to let her know that he had arrived safely in San Francisco and that he was missing her at least half as much as she was him.

Certain she would hear from him soon, she was reluctant to leave the hotel suite for fear she would miss his call. A trip to the local express-mail service couldn't be avoided, however, and the sooner the mail went out, the sooner she could join him in San Francisco.

Afterward Tara was sure that providence brought her there at the exact same time that one of Jonas's relatives was mailing a package.

"Why, thank you, Miss Miranda," the clerk chirped to the striking woman standing just in front of her at the counter. "Glad to hear that Ryan's home and back on his feet again. Nasty business that." The wizened little man shook his head to emphasize his dismay that anything so wicked could happen in their small town. "You have a nice day, you hear?"

"Thank you, Harvey," the woman responded in a soft cultured drawl.

Tara's ears perked up at the mention of Miranda's name. It had to be the aunt Jonas had bitterly referred to as the Queen of the Clan. After all, how many Mirandas could there be in a town this size? She studied the woman carefully. In her fifties, she could have easily passed for a much younger woman. Her blond hair was perfectly coiffed and her shapely figure had suffered little from the passage of time. Taking in her elegant Southwestern skirt and matching embroidered shirt, as well as the tasteful turquoise jewelry that she carried off with such casual grace, Tara found herself wishing she'd taken more care in choosing her own attire this morning. In jeans and an oversize T-shirt, she made quite a contrast to the regal matriarch of the Fortune family. The princess and the pauper, so to speak.

Laden with packages headed for their San Francisco office, Tara thought about simply pretending she had no interest whatsoever in this particular patron. Except that she did. A very personal interest that overrode any anxiety she might feel about her own appearance or inappropriate introduction to someone rich and famous.

Tara wiped her hands on her jeans. As the woman turned from the counter to leave, she stuck out her hand as if to stop her.

"Miranda Fortune?" she asked, her firm voice be-

lying her nervousness. "Allow me to introduce myself. I'm Tara Summers."

Miranda graciously took Tara's hand, but it was
clear from the confused look on her face that she had
no idea who Tara was. Disappointment coursed
through Tara. Had it been too much to hope that Jonas
had, at the very least, mentioned her to his relatives?

"I'm Jonas Goodfellow's—"

What exactly *was* she in relation to him? Neither
wife nor fiancée. She wondered if she should just
blurt out that she was his lover.

"Assistant," Tara finished.

Blue eyes the exact same captivating shade as
Jonas's lit up at the name. She took Tara by the elbow
and steered her away from the counter and an overly
curious clerk.

"Jonas?" she repeated. "My dear, do you perhaps
have any influence over my headstrong nephew?"

"I'd like to think so," Tara stammered as Miranda
directed Harvey to "take care of this young lady's
things while we have a little chat."

Luckily there was no one else around so they had
relative privacy, though Tara could see the clerk
straining to overhear their conversation. She was glad
when an incoming phone call distracted him.

"Ryan tells me that Jonas has left town," Miranda
said.

Tara nodded her head. She doubted whether anything escaped the scrutiny of this woman's vivid gaze.

"I can't tell you how badly we all feel about what
happened to poor Jonas. Of course, from our perspective it was perfectly natural to jump to the conclusion that he was somehow involved in the plot to

murder my brother—seeing as how he did bring the wine that was later found to be poisoned.''

Tara's eyes flashed fire and she rushed to his defense. ''It hurt him terribly that you could think him capable of such a crime. I'll have you know that Jonas is the kindest, gentlest man that ever—''

Miranda interrupted her with a wave of her jeweled hand. ''Personally I always did think that there was something funny in the way things went down. It all seemed too neat, and I never could come up with a believable motive for Jonas to want to do in poor Ryan, who's done nothing but try to right the wrongs of our brother's sordid past.''

Tara would never have guessed that Miranda would be such an up-front regular sort of person. Despite everything Jonas had said about her, it was hard not to like her. Everything from her firm handshake to her direct gaze to her open honest discussion made Tara instinctively feel she could trust this woman, whom she guessed to be about the same age her mother would have been had she lived. Emboldened by a gut feeling, she swallowed hard before venturing into personal territory.

''Why would you want to give Jonas money just for being related to you?''

Hoping it didn't make her sound like a gold digger, she regretted asking the question the second it was out of her mouth. Still, she wondered if there was a polite way to explain that Jonas assumed the offer was bogus.

''It seems the least we could do for each of Cameron's lost heirs. I understand that Jonas had a hard time of it as a boy growing up. It breaks my heart to think of any child feeling unloved. Abandoned.''

Something about that particular word caused Miranda's voice to crack. Her eyes clouded over with such pain that Tara couldn't help wondering if she was speaking from personal angst.

She decided to be as honest as possible under the circumstances. "Jonas is scarred by his past," she explained, "and angry at the way his newfound family jumped to the conclusion he's a killer. Quite frankly he doesn't believe your offer is genuine."

Tara paused, considering the full responsibility of relaying someone else's feelings. "And to be honest, even if it is, I'm not sure it will bring him any closer to the Fortune family."

Miranda's crooked smile left little doubt that she found Jonas's stubbornness a rather endearing quality, one that the Fortunes might actually value. "Luckily that's not a condition of the trust that Mary Ellen and I established. We have no intention of trying to bind someone to us with money. Believe me, I know first-hand that it won't work."

The more Tara talked to this woman, the more intriguing she became. She was just as complex and fascinating as her nephew.

Miranda offered her another warm smile. "The next time you talk to Jonas, please assure him that the offer is bona fide and that it comes without any strings attached. Really. Of course, that's not to say that we all wouldn't dearly love to welcome him back into the fold. Anything you can do, my dear, toward that end would be most appreciated."

Tara felt breathless. If the rest of the Fortune family was anything like this woman, Jonas would be a fool to let his wounded pride keep him from the kind of love and support he'd been longing for all of his life.

"You understand, of course, that it will take some time to establish the trust and release the money to each of the heirs. Legal matters can be so time-consuming, you know."

Tara wasn't nearly as concerned about the legalities of the trust fund as she was about Jonas's well-being.

"Do you know of any other leads in the attempted-murder case?" she asked. "You all must be terrified, with the real culprit still on the loose."

Miranda's smile faded. "Actually I did hear some disturbing news that you might want to pass on to Jonas if he shows any interest at all in our conversation. I ran into my ex-husband's widow in San Antonio. She's working at a boutique there and happened to let it slip that Lloyd's estate is bankrupt. Not that I'm jumping to any conclusions, mind you, but both Lloyd and Leeza were at the reunion, and as far as motives go, it seems to me that they…"

Not wanting to verbalize any unconfirmed suspicions, Miranda let her words trail off before changing the subject. "Why don't you come out to the ranch and have dinner with me this weekend?" Miranda suggested. "We could talk in private and get to know one another better."

Though flattered, Tara had no choice but to refuse the invitation. "I'm leaving for San Francisco tomorrow," she said. "But I promise to pass on your kind sentiments to Jonas and to do everything in my power to see he gives the Fortunes a second chance. If the rest of the family is anything like you, I'd hate to see him miss the opportunity to get to know you all a lot better."

"That's kind of you to say. Are you sure you

couldn't book a later flight?'' Miranda asked. "I'd truly love to introduce you to the rest of the family.''

"I have to get back to Jonas as soon as possible.''

"Ah,'' Miranda replied with a knowing smile. "You've got it bad, don't you. Don't bother answering. The way you feel is written all over your lovely face. I just hope my nephew knows what a jewel he has in you.''

"Me, too,'' Tara admitted with a wistful little sigh.

Miranda pulled a gold pen and a blank card out of her purse. Hastily writing down a number, she pressed the card into Tara's hand and patted it reassuringly. "It's my phone number. Feel free to call anytime. And please, do all you can to assure Jonas that we truly want him in our family in more than name alone.''

Tara had unexpected tears in her eyes as she left the store. Never would she have guessed how warm and welcoming the Fortunes could be. For some reason the meeting with Miranda made her miss her own mother terribly. Perhaps it was due to the graciousness with which Miranda had treated her. How she missed such a maternal presence in her life! Since her mother had passed away, Tara had been left with the burden of raising two irresponsible brothers and taking care of a father adrift in his grief and too ill to find much pleasure in life.

It was little wonder that Jonas was so deeply hurt when it appeared the Fortunes had turned on him. It must have been like losing Christmas after glimpsing it for the first time from inside the window rather than observing it longingly from the outside. Tara could hardly wait to get back to her room and tell him what she'd heard straight from his aunt's mouth.

Undaunted by the fact that he'd left no message whatsoever for her at the hotel, she took it upon herself to call him. Sounding even farther away than the long-distance call warranted, his response to her version of the conversation she'd had with his aunt Miranda was pessimistic, to say the least.

"Sweetheart, don't let them bamboozle you like they did me," he warned. "If a mule kicks me once, it's the mule's fault..."

"But if he kicks you twice, it's your fault," she finished in an exasperated tone. "We're not talking mules here, Jonas. We're talking about family."

"Other than Ellen, I don't have any family," he replied shortly, not bothering to even mention his estranged stepfather.

"The point is that you could. From what I saw of your aunt Miranda today, you'd be crazy to turn your back on what they have to offer you."

The stony silence on the other end of the line was intended to let Tara know she had overstepped the boundaries of what he was willing to accept as well-intended advice.

Tara didn't care. Her gut feeling told her she was right. "What reason would she have to lie to me? I can't believe you're being so bullheaded."

"And I can't believe you're so gullible to believe that anyone is going to willingly give that much money away without expecting something in return— say, a firstborn son or my very soul!"

"Gullible!" Tara sputtered in hurt indignation.

It was their first official spat, and she had never suspected that name-calling would come so easily to either of them.

"Gullible...and sweet," came a tender admission from miles and miles away.

Like chocolate heated over a flame, Tara felt herself melting on the spot.

"And trusting," Jonas continued. "Way too trusting. Please try to understand that despite dear Auntie Miranda's gold-engraved invitation back to the fold, I've washed my hands of the Fortune family forever."

Though Tara objected to the snide tone Jonas used in referring to his aunt, he allowed her no chance to offer further protest.

"And if that disinherits me from the false promise of sudden wealth, it's my decision, not yours. Do you understand?"

"I understand all right," Tara countered, refusing to be intimidated. "I just don't have to respect it. I hope you're as understanding about my decision to continue searching to find the real culprit who tried to poison your uncle. With or without your help."

She had to hold the phone away from her ear to lessen the volume of the angry torrent of words spewing forth.

"I shouldn't have to remind you not to do anything stupid on my account!" Jonas fumed.

Suddenly all the resentments that had been building up inside Tara spilled over like a boiling pot too long unattended. In all the time they had worked together, she couldn't ever recall a time that Jonas had raised his voice at her. She didn't see how becoming his lover should grant him such a liberty now.

"And I shouldn't have to remind you not to yell at me! Or that I don't need your permission to lead my life as I see fit," she snapped just before severing the connection.

* * *

"Must have been cut off somehow," Jonas mumbled, punching in the number of the hotel.

The phone in the suite was busy. Off the hook more likely, he realized with a start. Perhaps he had been too forceful in his objection to her playing junior detective, but that certainly didn't give Tara the right to so rudely cut him off in midsentence. Never in all his life had he felt such a surge of fierce protectiveness well up in his being as when she had so blithely suggested putting herself in danger. For him. Like he was some pantywaist who couldn't take care of himself. Just because he had been eager to leave bitter memories of Red Rock behind didn't mean he was running away as Tara had so pointedly implied.

Did it?

The possibility gave him reason to pause. He hoped Tara didn't think him incapable of solving his own problems. He may not be the kind of muscle-bound hero portrayed in popular action films, but he wasn't exactly a slouch in the testosterone department. That a fragile young woman somehow felt the need to "save" him hurt his male pride. For pity's sake, he was the one who was supposed to rescue her.

From jail when she was just a wide-eyed teenager.

From a life of minimum-wage poverty.

From the drudgery of taking care of her ailing father and sacrificing her health for his.

But deep in his heart, Jonas knew that the real question was who was going to rescue her from him.

He missed her terribly. More than he ever could have imagined. More than he wanted to admit. The fact that he hadn't called her was an act of supreme willpower designed to prove to himself that she hadn't taken up permanent residence in his heart. That she had actually hung up on him without even letting him know when she was going to be joining him in San Francisco was more than simply irritating. It was agonizing.

That she took the phone off the hook just to spite him was insufferable.

Jonas had known it was a mistake to kiss Tara. He had compounded the problem by making love to her, foolishly hoping that doing so would satisfy his curiosity, slake his thirst and get her out of his system once and for all.

Never had he been so completely wrong on every count before.

Ever since he'd gotten on that plane back in San Antonio, he could think of nothing else but the enchanting woman he'd left behind. Right in the middle of a business transaction today he had experienced an erotic flashback: caught a glimpse of creamy flesh, heard a provocative little moan, imagined her hands all over his body. The next thing he knew the person sitting across from him was clearing his throat and looking at him strangely. With a start, Jonas realized that he was supposed to respond to a question he hadn't even heard.

"Enough of this nonsense!" he told himself, tossing the phone across the room and whacking it against the wall. He was too world-wise to be experiencing such overwhelming adolescent feelings. And too deeply buried in denial to examine those feelings very closely.

While there was no way to undo what he'd done to Tara in stripping her of her virginity, he could certainly do his best to put his life back on the carefully laid-out fast track he'd so painstakingly laid out. Besides, it wasn't fair to tie such a vibrant pure woman to a heart as jaded as his. Tara deserved a love complete with roses and poetry and serenades. She deserved a husband who worked from nine to five, was home every evening and weekend and wanted to put down permanent roots.

Jonas was not such a man. Even if Miranda's preposterous offer was genuine, the Fortune money would simply enable him to travel more, not less. There was much of the world left that he had yet to explore.

And much of his heart that he intended to leave uncharted.

To make matters worse, Tara had made it clear that she eventually wanted children. Apparently a houseful. The thought of her surrounded by a brood of noisy kids made Jonas smile despite himself. She would be a wonderful mother. Just because he had no desire ever to become a parent shouldn't give him the right to deprive her of the opportunity.

Or of marriage, for that matter.

Failing in a relationship wasn't exactly like taking a risk in business. One couldn't declare a heart bankrupt or cover up emotional scars with a promising spreadsheet. Jonas hadn't gotten where he was in his profession by letting his feelings dominate his brain. His mother's life of self-sacrifice had shown him how dangerous it was to base lifetime decisions on emotions alone, no matter how noble they might be. He had told Tara up-front that he didn't consider himself the marrying kind. Sex was a natural part of his life, but he certainly wasn't about to let it drive all his decisions.

He knew, of course, that Tara didn't see things his way. A creature of passion and ideals, she saw the world in fairy-tale terms. He hoped she came to her senses before she grew old waiting for her father to stop using her, waiting for a knight in shining armor to rescue her.

He was not that knight.

When Tara returned to San Francisco, he determined, in what he considered a most chivalrous manner, not to succumb to his physical desire for her again. Without the kind of commitment he was unable to give, it simply wasn't fair to her. They would just have to put the past behind them and do their level best to carry on with business as usual.

He was certain Tara would understand that he was only doing it in her best interest...

Seven

——

Tara didn't seem to recall Nancy Drew ever having as much trouble piecing together clues as she was. When her leads all turned cold after a series of fruitless phone calls, she was glad she hadn't given up her day job to become a private eye on a full-time basis. Sheriff Grayhawk had been pleasant but firm when she had offered to help him on the case. He thanked her for her interest, then politely sent her on her way with the same admonition as Jonas had about needing to leave police business to qualified professionals.

Luckily just the thought of being with Jonas again soon was enough to take much of the sting out of Tara's failed stint as a detective. She hadn't known it was possible to miss anyone so much. The past few days had been the most miserable of her life. Dozens of times a day, she found herself staring off into space, every cell in her body straining with longing as she recalled the most intimate details of their relationship. The passage of time hadn't done anything but burn the memory of their lovemaking more deeply into her very being.

Though still bothered by the harsh words they had exchanged over the phone, Tara came to the realization that Jonas's stubborn pride wasn't nearly as insurmountable as she might have believed at the time.

All that really mattered was being together again.

Making an executive decision, Tara booked a reservation on the next flight out of San Antonio, then turned her hotel key in to the front desk. She counted herself fortunate in avoiding a speeding ticket for racing across the open Texas plains on the way to the airport. Her heart may have been light at the thought of rejoining her lover, but it had the opposite effect on the foot she applied to the accelerator.

Determined to catch Jonas at the Emporium, which was the name he'd given the business that had started out as a small warehouse outlet and become one of the finest merchandising stores in the city, before the workday ended, she changed into the pink suit he said he liked so much. She entertained bold thoughts of meeting him wearing nothing but a trench coat, but wasn't sure either one of them was ready for that level of playfulness yet in their relationship. Tara smiled. She would never have guessed that her newly discovered sexuality would be zooming ahead at the speed of light.

The two-and-a-half-hour plane ride seemed an interminable amount of time. Back at long last in San Francisco again, Tara retrieved her car from long-term parking and headed straight for the Emporium

and Jonas's arms. Slipping quietly inside the back
door, she lingered a moment over the sight of him at
work. Broad-shouldered in a cable-knit sweater well
suited for the early-autumn chill blowing in off the
harbor, he looked so fine that the sight stole her
breath. He was on the phone with his back to her,
and she noticed that his thick dark hair was in need
of a professional trim. That Jonas relied on her to
make such personal appointments for him had always
made her feel special.

He sounded frazzled, a fact confirmed by the muf-
fled word he used to describe the caller after hanging
up the phone.

"Has anyone ever told you that your telephone
skills leave something to be desired?" Tara asked
him.

Jonas wheeled around at the sound of the soft sultry
voice. Fire leaped to his eyes at the sight of her walking across the room. He jumped to his feet.

"You're back," he said simply.

Then as if realizing how unnecessary and hope-
lessly stupid the observation was, he added, "I'm
glad. It's been hell without you."

Tara had been dreaming of this moment ever since
she boarded the plane earlier that day. It seemed to
her that the entire world was encompassed in the distance separating them. Even the dust mites dancing
in the shaft of light passing through the window
seemed molecularly charged in the look that bonded
them as lovers. Oh, how Tara had missed those blue
blue eyes, that handsome rugged face and the deep
rumbling voice.

She was relieved to discover that Jonas *was* glad
to see her, after all.

How she managed to keep from vaulting over counters filled with exquisite objects and literally throwing herself into his arms was a credit to her self-control. Making a conscious effort to move gracefully across the room, she told her tripping heart that she would get there soon enough step by steady step. Jonas came out from behind a desk that suddenly took on new appeal at the unbidden thought of wiping it clean with the sweep of an arm and making passionate love on its scarred surface.

"You'd better brace yourself," Tara warned him seductively, taking notice of the way he was gripping the edge of the desk with both hands behind him.

If he was worried that she was still angry with him, Tara was eager to put his mind at ease. Wreathing her arms around his neck, she zeroed in on his lips, determined to kiss him until he was as weak with wanting as she.

She cursed the tinkling sound of a bell announcing the arrival of a customer. Jonas turned his head and deflected Tara's kiss with his cheek.

"Not in the office," he reproached her softly, unwinding her arms from around him.

While there was no denying that part of him wanted nothing more than to stay in those gentle loving arms forever, another part of him felt trapped. There was no other word for it, Jonas realized. Until he had a chance to sort out his feelings and figure out how he was going to continue working with this woman on a professional basis, the confirmed bachelor in him desperately needed to put some space between them. The glint in her eyes made him feel like Frankenstein. The sweet young woman he had so recently deflowered had been transformed into a nymphomaniac. Not that he minded that nearly as much as the worry that she seemed to expect marriage and babies from him.

"Not in the office?" Tara parroted in disbelief.

She looked as if he had just slapped her across the face. Stepping back, she numbly allowed Jonas to slip past her.

As far as Tara was concerned, he could darn well deal with customers himself. *She* certainly wasn't about to, not with tears blurring her vision.

"Yes, sir," she snapped with a mock salute, surprised the words could find their way around the thick lump in her throat.

It always seemed business was most brisk right before closing time. Burying herself in bookkeeping for the remainder of the afternoon, Tara let Jonas attend to the late-day rush of customers demanding his attention. All her sweet dreams of being swept into his arms and rushing off to bed had dissolved with the jingle of a bell. Tara swore she would rip the blasted thing off the door the second the Closed sign was posted in the window.

Granted things were hectic, but she couldn't help but feel as if Jonas was deliberately avoiding her. When he had said he'd missed her, she hadn't thought he'd been referring to the mess the office had become in her absence. She wasn't so sure now. Taking comfort in the familiarity of work, which helped to calm her, Tara nonetheless marked every minute's passing.

When the last customer had left and the workday was officially at a close, Jonas found her with her head bent over her desk, pretending to be unaware of just how late it was.

"Quitting time," he announced, coming to stand beside her desk.

"And what exactly are we quitting?" she asked quietly.

Jonas tensed. A cocker spaniel pup had nothing on those big brown eyes of hers shimmering with pain. An invisible hand grabbed his heart and squeezed hard. He rebelled against the guilt rising inside him. What idiot ever coined the expression about love and marriage going together like a horse and carriage? Obviously someone from the horse-and-buggy era. From his perspective, the single life offered a man far more freedom and less financial risk than marriage. What he really needed to do, Jonas realized, was to sit down and discuss this with Tara like reasonable adults. Away from the office.

"Work. What else would I be talking about quitting, Tara? What do you say I take you out to dinner to celebrate your homecoming?"

The relief in her lovely features was indisputable. Tension slipped from her shoulders as she offered him a tentative smile.

"Sounds great. Just let me grab my purse."

A veteran of failed relationships, Jonas knew just the place to take her to avoid a tearful scene if Tara decided he was being unreasonable and rejected his offer of continuing on as they were—with no strings attached. When she had first made her presence known earlier in the day, looking so pretty and undeniably happy to see him, Jonas allowed himself to wonder for a brief shining moment if life couldn't really be so simple: beginning and ending his days in the arms of a good and gentle woman who really loved him for who he was. For an instant he actually considered locking the door and making love to her right there in the store on top of the massive desk he'd brought back from one of his trips into the outback of Australia. Such thoughts certainly didn't do much for his resolve. Such thoughts were definitely bad for business.

Remembering his promise to put his lust aside and do what was best for Tara, he vowed to let her go and make a life with a man not so scarred by the past nor so jaundiced toward the future. The present was all that counted for men as hardened as Jonas fancied himself. Need he remind himself that such men didn't put stock in happily-ever-afters?

The sooner Tara came to understand that, the better off they both would be.

Jonas suggested dinner at a nearby sports bar that was the least-romantic place he could think of. The ocean air put twin roses in Tara's cheeks that matched that amazing pink suit of hers. How could such a professional-looking outfit make her look so desirable? Jonas couldn't help but contrast this stroll along busy streets with the one they had taken the evening they spent in Red Rock's quaint city park. A skateboarder whizzed past, knocking Tara right into Jonas.

His arm shot protectively around her. She looked up at him, her gentle eyes filling with hope that he might just succumb to his desire to stop walking long enough to kiss her right there in front of God and throngs of strangers. That he had been disinclined earlier to do just that in the shop in front of a smattering of customers clearly should have been far less important than her tender feelings.

"Are you all right?" he asked her.

Though Tara nodded her head, her eyes couldn't

lie. Clearly she was far from all right as she continued the brisk pace Jonas set. There was no hand-holding as there had been in Red Rock. No picket fences to trail sticks along in a lively country beat. No children running the streets. No Civil War cannons reminding of the mistakes of the past. Only garish window fronts demanding that the whims of the present be satisfied immediately.

The bar seemed as raucous as the streets outside. Jonas jostled his way to a small table in back and ordered himself a beer and a white wine for Tara.

"We need to talk," he said.

Tara strained to hear him. He couldn't have picked a less-private spot.

"What?"

"About the office," he hollered across the table. "We have to remember that the office is not a place to display personal feelings."

Tara indicated that she still couldn't hear him. Jonas scooted his chair next to hers and put his mouth next to her ear and repeated himself. He couldn't help but notice how fragrant her hair smelled and how incredibly soft it felt against his cheek. He fought the urge to nibble her earlobe. To nuzzle her neck. To suckle her breast. To sweep her up like some savage and ravage her.

Tara dropped her hand to his lap and gave him a clandestine seductive squeeze. Hoping to get him out of this strange funk, she intended to beguile him with charm and inviting bedroom eyes.

Jonas groaned at her blatant sexual advance. The sorrow in his heart at the thought of what he had to do made him ache more than the fullness in his groin. Damn, but she was making this hard!

He removed her hand and placed it on top of the table. "I said we need to talk," he hollered.

Tara grinned. It seemed strange that she was the playful one and he suddenly so inhibited.

She was no fool. Obviously the poor man was having second thoughts. As much as that pained her, Tara wasn't about to be dissuaded by it. Although Jonas had made her no promises, there was no doubt in her mind that he cared deeply for her. She wanted to believe, needed to believe, that he loved her and would someday come to realize that he wanted to marry her, as well. Still she was not so naive as to believe that men thought making love automatically led to marriage. Her mother had always maintained that men don't invest the same emotional commitment that women do in making love.

Nonetheless Tara knew that Jonas had been moved by the experience. So much so that it terrified him. She just had to figure out a way to allay his worries without losing him in the process.

She held up her hand as if being required to take an official oath.

"I solemnly swear that I won't come on to you at the office. No winking, kissing or flirting of any kind. If that's what you're sure you want…"

Suddenly Jonas wasn't so sure it was.

"It is," he said.

"So tell me," Tara asked him with a mischievous twinkle in her eye, "how exactly am I supposed to act around you?"

He hastened to elucidate. "Just like before, of course."

"And out of the office?" she queried, leaning close

Play the

"LAS

3 FRE

FREE GIFTS!

1. Pull back all 3 tabs on th
   see what we have for you
   FREE!

2. Send back this card and
   novels. These books have
   $4.50 each in Canada, bu

3. There's no catch. You're
   nothing — ZERO — for
   any minimum number of

4. The fact is, thousands of r
   the Silhouette Reader Serv
   delivery...they like getting
   they're available in stores.
   featuring author news, ho

5. We hope that after receivin
   subscriber. But the choice
   all! So why not take us up
   You'll be glad you did!

FREE!
No Obligation to Buy!
No Purchase Necessary!

Play the
"LAS VEGAS"
Game

YES! I have pulled back the 3 tabs. Please send me all the free Silhouette Desire® books and the gift for which I qualify. I understand that I am under no obligation to purchase any books, as explained on the back and opposite page.

326 SDL DFSN   **225 SDL DFSP**
(S-D-OS-10/01)

NAME   (PLEASE PRINT CLEARLY)

ADDRESS

APT.#   CITY

STATE/PROV.   ZIP/POSTAL CODE

GET 2 FREE BOOKS & A FREE MYSTERY GIFT!

GET 2 FREE BOOKS!

GET 1 FREE BOOK!

TRY AGAIN!

If offer card is missing write to: Silhouette Reader Service, 3010 Walden Ave., P.O. Box 1867, Buffalo, NY 14240-1867

BUSINESS REPLY MAIL

FIRST-CLASS MAIL   PERMIT NO. 717-003   BUFFALO, NY

POSTAGE WILL BE PAID BY ADDRESSEE

SILHOUETTE READER SERVICE
3010 WALDEN AVE
PO BOX 1867
BUFFALO NY 14240-9952

NO POSTAGE
NECESSARY
IF MAILED
IN THE
UNITED STATES

to him and whispering in his ear. "Tell me how you want me to act out of the office."

Jonas was having a hard time thinking, let alone responding verbally. In a war between mind and body, the flesh had certain advantages. Blood was pumping through his veins in hot spurts that left him at a loss for words.

"Like my associate—and friend."

Tara raised a teasing eyebrow. "Just how friendly are you talking?"

Clearly she was having great sport at his expense. She knew that he wanted her as badly as she wanted him and thought to use her feminine wiles to keep him as docile as a puppy.

"Cut it out," he said loudly enough to startle her. The hurt look on her face indicated that she found his continued resistance to her overtures losing all its flirtatious charm fast. "I want to make sure that you didn't get the wrong idea back in Red Rock."

Tara's mouth dropped open. Surely he wasn't about to demean the time they had spent together in the most intimate of ways.

"The wrong idea?" she repeated slowly, testing the words on her tongue as one would a foreign dish. "Exactly what kind of wrong ideas do you think I have that need to be straightened out?"

Sorry now that he hadn't picked a quieter place, after all, Jonas found he hated admitting his feelings with a raised voice. He knew it made him sound unintentionally angry and harsh.

"You know that I care for you, Tara. It's just that I'm afraid I might have misled you about my intentions."

It sounded as stilted as a line out of an old black-

and-white movie. Tara, however, wasn't wringing her hands the way the actresses did in such films when their honor had been besmirched. She didn't slap his face or mention that he had sullied her or burst into tears demanding that he marry her. Instead, she just sat there, looking like a cool pink rosebud in that tailored all-too-feminine suit, quietly sipping her wine, looking over her glass at him as if he was losing control of all his senses.

Which he most definitely was. His palms were sweating, his heart felt like an elephant was using it as a welcome mat, and his lung capacity seemed to have shrunk to that of a very old man's. Despite all that, his traitorous flesh had the audacity to react to this woman as if she had just consented to lie beneath him once again.

Oh, sweet thought!

Jonas had to wonder if he wasn't completely mad to throw away such sensual bliss all in the name of gallantry. He wished there were some way of explaining that his intentions in trying to let her go without somehow insulting her were actually honorable.

Tara set her drink down. "What exactly are your intentions, Jonas? To pretend that what happened between us didn't? To put this all behind us and simply go on with business as usual?"

As if fearing that she was going to inflict some harm on him, he flinched as she reached up and put a hand to his cheek. The skin along his jawline tingled where she trailed her fingertips tenderly. He shivered, fighting the need to feel her silky skin against his own. Wanting her with an intensity he hadn't known before, Jonas was sorely tempted to take her on his own terms—as he had so many women before her who had used him for their own purposes, as well. To give pleasure and take pleasure when it was offered without compunction was not something that he had been above in the past.

But not with Tara. For some inexplicable reason he couldn't be so coldhearted with this particular woman. However, if they were to maintain any kind of relationship, he wanted to make damned sure that there was no question as to the terms of their arrangement.

Eight

"I'm more than willing to continue where we left off in Red Rock," Jonas informed her. "I just want to make sure you understand that I'm not asking you to marry me. I've tried to make it perfectly clear that marriage is not in my future. Personally I don't see you agreeing to that kind of arrangement, but right now it's the only offer on the table."

Tara shook her head as if stunned that he would approach her about such a matter as if it was some common business transaction. Had she not invested her heart in this relationship, she might well have done exactly what it appeared Jonas wanted her to do: stomp off and let him revert back to the emotionally stunted state in which she had found him. Had she not loved him so much, she would have given up on him as a lost cause. As it was, Tara knew that

)

Jonas was merely reacting to his frightening new feelings the only way he knew how—by running away.

It was a pattern she recognized well. Whenever she got too close, he typically bolted for some foreign destination under the pretense of a necessary buying venture. As nothing more than a loyal friend and assistant in the past, she had been forced to accept his behavior, childish though it may have been. As his lover, however, she wasn't about to let him pull that same back-door routine on her ever again.

"Jonas, what happened between us was the most beautiful thing that I've ever experienced, and I have no intention whatsoever of ever forgetting it. Quite frankly I'll be surprised if you can, either. Just in case you're not aware of it, I'll say it again. I love you and, of course, I want to marry you. I'd be lying if I said otherwise, but we can play this out any way you want. You're the man I want."

A man definitely worth waiting for, she thought to herself, counting the years she had already invested in him and already disenchanted with the idea of looking for anyone else to take his place in her heart.

Jonas might very well think that marriage was out of the question, but Tara had come from a long line of women who didn't shy away from a challenge. If Jonas thought his cold offer of premarital sex without strings was going to scare her off, he had another think coming. True, it hurt her deeply that he would suggest such an arrangement. Still, she was not about to give up on this man simply because he was afraid to invest in an emotional commitment. She felt sure that she could eventually convince him to change his mind.

Dropping her hand from his face, she donned an

enigmatic smile that would have made the Mona Lisa jealous. "In case you haven't noticed, I'm very good at waiting when it suits my purposes," she told him evenly.

There was a slim possibility that the evening could have been salvaged had Tara not insisted on going where even angels dared to tread. Having grown tired of Jonas's stubborn pride where his newly found family was concerned and emboldened by the bravado that she had shown in refusing to be cowed by his professed fear of commitment, she decided to broach the topic of her conversation with his aunt over cocktails.

"I think you should give Miranda a call," she said, pulling the phone number that she had been given out of her wallet and pushing it across the table at him.

"And I think you should stop worrying about things that don't concern you," he replied curtly.

Stung, Tara shoved the scrap of paper back into her purse, vowing to not let him see how deeply his words hurt her. That he was a man more comfortable hacking down jungles than building personal relationships was a given. Jonas was understandably prickly when it came to his family. Still, Tara suspected that the only way to dismiss the nagging fear that somewhere between California and Texas the man she loved had misplaced his feelings for her was to bring all his feelings out in the open. No matter how painful they may be.

Earlier she had told him that she was good at waiting, and she was. There was, however, a limit to her patience, and at the moment Jonas was testing it severely. Deliberately, she suspected. Though she was doing her best not to let it show on the surface, her nerves were beginning to fray. No matter how much she cared for him, she was not about to consent to being his emotional punching bag for life.

"What's wrong with me worrying about you?" she asked, setting her drink down and looking him directly in the eye. "I love you, for God's sake. Even though you haven't been able to say the same to me, I trust that someday you might just allow yourself the opportunity to love somebody, too. If not me, at least the family who has offered to pay for your attention!"

Jonas's eyes darkened to the color of polished gunmetal. Startled that she would dare speak to him in such a manner, he saw in an instant the opportunity to nip in the bud a relationship that was becoming too stifling for his professed lifestyle.

"Who asked you to be my caretaker?" he asked, measuring his words carefully. He was neither in the market for marriage nor a roommate. Nor did he want advice on personal matters. All he wanted was his freedom and an occasional romp between the sheets without any sticky emotional attachments and fear of becoming a father. If Tara wanted more than that from him, she was deluding herself. He didn't know how to say it more plainly.

"Don't you have enough on your hands already what with all the stray dogs and cats you take in, not to mention your poor ailing father, without sacrificing the rest of your life for a man like me? My mother, God rest her soul, already made that blood offering on my behalf, and to be honest, I didn't appreciate it. In fact, I resented the hell out of it. Take my advice and don't make the same mistake she did. In other words, I'd appreciate it if you'd live your own life and keep your pretty nose out of my business!''

The viciousness of the attack was unexpected. His words hit harder than a fist. Tara refused to allow the tears pooling in her eyes the freedom to fall down her cheeks. Silently she vowed that Jonas would never know the power he had to wound her. She hadn't imagined him capable of such callousness.

Anger lifted her chin defiantly in the air. She had been a fool to think she could ever be more to him than a convenient bedfellow and a loyal employee.

How dare he ridicule the love she felt for her family and upbraid her for showing concern about him! Pride alone kept her from throwing her drink in his face. If Jonas thought he had the ability to make her have a full-scale meltdown in public, he misjudged the metal in her spine. Taking a tiny sip of her drink, Tara pretended an aloofness she did not feel. The wine went down her throat like shards of glass.

Angry that she could make him feel like such a complete creep without saying a word, Jonas lashed out again. ''Just because we slept together doesn't mean I have to marry you,'' he told her.

''Who asked you to?'' Tara snapped, jumping to her feet in outrage. To be so publicly humiliated was more than any woman deserved. Throwing her napkin down on the table, she added in a hiss, ''Your ego knows no bounds.''

Jonas stood up, too, and raised his voice to be heard over the din in the room. ''One more thing. I don't want children, either. I don't even like kids!'' he hollered.

Tara didn't bother with theatrics. With quiet dignity, she excused herself to go to the ladies' room.

Having every intention of doing exactly what Jonas suggested and minding her own damned business for the rest of her life, she slipped out the front door. The August breeze blowing in off the harbor was cool. She wondered how long he would wait there before discovering that she'd left. Until his guilt got the better of him or the bartender threw him out, whichever came first, she hoped.

As she walked, Tara was unaware of the dramatic sweep of the suspension cables of the Golden Gate Bridge glistening against the terraced hills across the bay. The most panoramic view in the world couldn't take away the sense of humiliation propelling her down the street. Numb, she did not cry as she slowly made her way past the painted ladies of San Francisco, those elegant terraced Victorian houses famous for their gaudy color schemes and elaborate ornamentation. She scarcely felt the tug on her calf muscles as she hiked up and down the steep hills of the city, lamenting the loss of time invested in a dead-end relationship.

She regretted the years she had squandered. Years of catering to Jonas's every whim, whether it concerned the strength of his coffee, the tone of the letters she drafted for him or the meticulous manner in which she kept his books for so many years. Years of fashioning herself into whatever she thought Jonas wanted her to be. Years of neglecting her own needs and those of her family. Precious years spent like so many shiny dimes fed to an arcade game that was never going to pay out.

Clearly she had a decision to make. She could continue wasting her life waiting for Jonas to realize how lucky he was to have her love. Or she could accept the fact that he was never going to see her as anything more than a besotted secretary willing to endure anything he dished out just so long as she could remain close to him. Tired of chasing him and hurt by the words he had flung in her face like some dirty rag, Tara came to realize that she had too much respect for herself to continue waiting in the wings for him. Whether she wanted to accept it or not, he was never going to come to his senses and get down on one knee to propose marriage to her. If it survived at all, clearly theirs would have to be a relationship without a ring.

To be fair to him, he had warned her up-front that he was not the marrying kind. He had made her no promises. Nor even hinted that he wanted to continue an intimate relationship. Reading anything more than fantastic sex into the night of passion that they had shared was the epitome of wishful thinking. Obviously Jonas wanted nothing more than to put that night behind him and take up his old life where he had left off.

Too proud to continue begging for any scrap of affection that Jonas might toss her way, Tara decided that if life was a banquet, she was entitled to sit at the table and share in the feast.

Not merely to serve it.

Tara waited until she got home to allow herself a good healthy cry. Afterward, she began penning her resignation letter. His precious business was bound to run less smoothly without her taking care of all the mundane details that he couldn't be bothered with on a daily basis. As she wrote, a voice from the past called to her. It was her mother, repeating her oft-issued warning not to foolishly succumb to the pursuit of pleasure at the expense of commitment.

Her mother had been a wise woman, hoping to spare her daughter the grief that had wrapped itself around her like a shroud. What to Tara had been a rare and beautiful sharing of body and soul had been nothing more than great sex to Jonas. What was nothing less than a holy act of love to her had been nothing more than indiscriminate intercourse to him, dependent less on depth of emotion than willingness of the flesh.

Her mother's voice assured Tara that she could sit by the phone for eternity and Jonas wouldn't call. He was not going to ask her out for romantic dinners. Or buy her extravagant gifts. Or ask her to be his wife. Those were silly schoolgirl fantasies.

Still, despite her mother's pessimistic warnings, Tara could not bring herself to regret making love to Jonas. Although ill-fated, it had nonetheless been the most splendid time of her life.

So when the phone rang, Tara jumped. Hoping against hope that it was actually Jonas calling to salvage their relationship, she blew her nose and dried her tears. She didn't want him to know that she had been crying over him. Tara reached for the receiver with a quivering hand. Her initial disappointment that it was not Jonas at the other end quickly gave way to a sense of dread.

In the span of a single heartbeat, Jonas suddenly became the least of Tara's worries.

Nine

Tara held her father's hand to her cheek and thanked God for giving him a chance to survive the heart attack that had nearly claimed his life. On top of his blood condition, it was a miracle he had survived at all. Disgusted at herself for belaboring the state of her own heart when her daddy's had physically betrayed him, she vowed never again to let this good man down. Her father had once been such a big hearty man. It hurt to see him so old and frail. Aghast at how he looked hooked up to all manner of tubes and monitors, she tried to hide her tears from him. And vowed to make up for lost time with him. Here, at least, was a man who appreciated what she did for him. A man who would never fall from his pedestal like someone else she knew.

A man who wasn't afraid of wearing his heart out by loving too much.

"I quit my job today," she explained to her siblings without offering any explanation of her actions. "So there's no reason I can't take care of Dad while we both get back on our feet."

Although her brothers protested that such a sacrifice was unnecessary, no one wanted to see their father in a nursing home. Ultimately it took little arm-twisting to come to an agreement that Tara would move back home, at least until she found another job. Mike and Pat promised to clean out her apartment and transfer all her belongings to the three-story pink Victorian house where they had all been raised.

And so it was that just a short time later, she found herself setting a plate of toast in front of her father at their old kitchen table, telling him that everything was just fine. Just fine. Surely the fact that he had been dismissed from the hospital so quickly was a good sign.

As weak as he was, Howard Summers wasn't sure that he wanted his daughter waiting on him hand and foot—if it meant she had to stop living for herself.

"I may not be the man I once was," he said, holding out his cup to have his coffee refilled, "but I hope the sorry SOB who hurt you has better sense than to show up around here. I've still got my police-issue .357 you know, and I won't hesitate to use it if I thought it would bring you any satisfaction."

"I know, Daddy," she said, nibbling halfheartedly on a piece of toast. "If it's okay with you, I'll just hang around home and make sure you're on the mend while I figure out what I'm going to do with the rest of my life."

It was important that her father believed this arrangement was mutually beneficial, or he was sure to throw a fit about being treated like an invalid. Contrary to what Jonas believed, Howard Summers was just as adamant as he was about her not wasting her life on an old man. Blaming her lack of appetite on the sorry state of her heart, Tara abandoned her toast and focused on the wallpaper that was beginning to peel in the corner of the room. It so bothered her to see the old place in disrepair that she vowed to take the time to repaint and repaper while attempting to get her life back on course.

With her skills, background and natural ability, Tara assured her father that she wouldn't have any trouble finding regular employment. Of course, there was no way of knowing what it would pay. Likely nowhere near as well as her old job. Nor was it likely to give her the same sense of satisfaction. The truth was, Tara had always considered herself more of a partner to Jonas than a mere assistant.

Whatever job she found, Tara knew it would have one major benefit that her old job hadn't. It wouldn't carve her heart into pieces and serve it back to her on a silver platter. Her father was right about one thing. She did deserve better.

Still, giving up five years of hopes and dreams, not to mention her heart, was not an easy thing to do. Tara couldn't help but hope that Jonas was struggling some with her abrupt departure, as well.

He was.

Furious with her for ditching him at the sports bar, Jonas had called her apartment several times that night wanting to make sure that she had gotten home safely. There had been no answer. Remembering how she had hung up on him and taken the phone off the hook in Red Rock, he assumed that she was simply being obstinate again in her refusal to answer. Too proud to run after her, he'd decided to wait until Monday when she reported for work to have a word with her. That way they both would have time to calm down and think rationally.

That he was surprised she failed to show up for work that Monday was a tribute to her unwavering loyalty over the past five years. Customarily Tara arrived well before him, opened up the shop and had a perfect cup of coffee ready and waiting for him. When she still refused to answer his phone calls, Jonas slammed the receiver down in exasperation. He could damn well run the office and his life without her.

With the same determination with which he faced every obstacle in his life, Jonas proceeded to make the best of things. It wasn't easy. Aside from missing Tara's usual cheerful company, he had great difficulty simultaneously juggling his own work and her considerable duties. Dealing with demanding customers, pesky phone calls, paperwork and a guilty conscience all at the same time was enough to tempt him to simply hang the Closed sign in the window.

He was sorting through a stack of mail he had dropped on his desk when he discovered her letter of resignation. It was as neat, orderly and professional as the lady who had penned it.

At the sight of her bold signature, Jonas's heart plummeted. He knew that when the realization hit that Tara was truly gone, his heart was certain to shatter into a million shards.

Ripping the letter into shreds and tossing it into the trash, he tried bolstering himself with the knowledge that he had all the accruements of success: an expensive car, a flourishing business, an elegant condo with a view of the bay. All the things he'd been told he would never be able to obtain on his own. He had proved himself to the world with a business that exceeded even his own expectations. It most certainly surpassed his stepfather's prediction that he'd never amount to anything.

Everything about him screamed success. Why then, he wondered as he looked around at all that he had accomplished, did he feel so empty?

Was it because the pattern that had started at his birth was repeated as Jonas found himself once again abandoned and alone? Having made his place in the world, he fiercely reminded himself that nobody could take that away from him. The fact that his victory felt hollow made him realize how little good it did for a man to conquer the entire universe if he had no one with whom to share it.

He wondered if Tara was amusing herself at this very moment with thoughts of the chaos she had left in her wake. There was little point in pretending that he missed her merely as an employee. What he really missed was the sweet smell of her hair, the sound of her voice, the way her eyes crinkled at the corners when she smiled, the compassion with which she treated every single human being who crossed her path, the way she made him feel unbound from all earthly ties when they made love.

The way she made him strive to be a better man.

No matter. He wasn't about to go crawling back to her when she was the one who had walked out on him. His stepfather had tried to make him crawl and had failed. As had the fabulous Fortunes. Jonas Goodfellow didn't crawl for anyone. It was as simple as that.

Having done his damnedest to persuade Tara that he was not the right man for her, Jonas knew that what he *should* be feeling was a deep sense of relief. No more walking on eggshells around the office fighting the desire to claim her body and soul. No more wrestling with the concept of marriage when he was so dead set against the institution itself. No more trying to let her down easy. No more worrying about a baby conceived to immortalize a night of the most splendid passion imaginable. No matter how angry Tara was at him, she would be duty bound to tell him if she was pregnant. He couldn't fathom such an honorable woman doing otherwise.

Time was certain to cure the gnawing ache in his gut. Wasn't it?

As the weeks wore on and his chest continued throbbing painfully where his heart used to be, he began cursing Tara for leaving so abruptly and not even leaving a clue where she had gone. Her landlord had been no help. Jonas tried telling himself that it was her competence alone that he missed and swore at himself for leaving the business so vulnerable to her absence. He had often told Tara that she was irreplaceable, but hadn't really understood what an understatement that was. That he had taken her for granted was shamelessly obvious in hindsight.

Based on that alone, he knew it served him right to have to endure the parade of assistants he had hired in her wake. Only one had shown any real potential, but she fell so far short of Jonas's expectations that she had told him in no uncertain terms where he could put the coffeemaker that she apparently couldn't operate to his satisfaction. Before taking her leave, she pointed out that the biggest problem he had with her was that she was simply not her predecessor.

She was right, of course. The plain truth was that no one was ever going to measure up to Tara.

Ever.

With a blinding flash of insight, Jonas realized that he needed Tara for far more than just his business. He needed her to be whole himself. The truth had been within his grasp all along. Just because he had lacked any solid male role models growing up didn't invalidate their necessity in the world. Just because his father had abandoned him and his mother didn't mean he was necessarily going to abandon Tara someday. Or that he would be a bad father because of some faulty gene passed down from generation to generation.

Ashamed that he could have been so foolishly fettered to such childhood fears, he refused to be held back by the past any longer. It was the present that concerned him now. With the determination that marked all his business interactions, Jonas decided on a bold plan of action. All he had to do now was find Tara and explain to her what a dolt he was, beg for mercy and pray that she would give him another chance.

For a man who had managed the most primitive inroads of uncharted jungles, Jonas figured it shouldn't be too hard to find the most beautiful blonde in the world carrying his heart around on a stake.

She was pregnant.

Tara rested her forehead on the cool porcelain of

the commode and waited for this latest wave of nausea to pass. The fact that she had been losing weight had confused her at first, but she could no longer continue to deny the truth. Looking at one's future from the bathroom floor somehow made everything unmistakably clear.

More than a month had passed since she had last seen Jonas. Luckily, Tara was made of sterner stuff than Jonas's mother. Unlike Leena Goodfellow, she was a strong and independent woman, who while not yet used to the idea of being a single mother, was not completely terrified by the thought either. It wasn't going to be easy raising a child by herself, but Tara knew she could handle it. Of course, there were options available to her that had not been legal when Jonas was born, but Tara already cherished the baby growing so secretively in her that no one would be able to guess her condition for quite some time. Despite the fact that she doubted whether Jonas would even want to know about the baby's existence, she would never consider aborting his child. Nor adopting it out, either, though she had to wonder if she wasn't being selfish, if it wouldn't be in the child's best interest to be raised in a two-parent family.

Right or wrong, however, Tara was keeping Jonas's baby.

She intended to cherish the product of their love— the only part of Jonas she got to keep. One could only wonder if his mother had ever tried contacting Cameron Fortune and, at the very least, informing him that their coupling had produced an heir. Jonas assumed that Leena had, but Tara could understand why she might not have.

Jonas's mother might have acted more out of love

for a man she couldn't have by choosing to raise his child alone rather than destroy his marriage. Tara was certain such a thought would be repugnant to Jonas, who liked casting Cameron Fortune as the clear-cut villain in the melodrama of his past. Tara knew life wasn't that black and white. Love was a fickle maiden, making it impossible for anyone to discern her motives.

Given his background, it was practically guaranteed that Jonas would feel obligated to accept the child as his. Likely he would insist on it, doing to Tara exactly what he perceived the Fortunes were attempting to do to him: throwing money at a problem to assuage their guilt. Out of a sense of obligation, he would likely offer to marry her in hopes of preventing another bastard child from growing up without his rightful father's name.

Rather than filling Tara with relief, the thought only saddened her.

While she knew many good marriages had been based on less, she wanted more. More than just a name for her baby. More than a big house or the kind of financial security Jonas's business could give their child or the money the Fortunes promised to bestow on him. Despite what anyone else thought, she knew that there were some things money could not buy, and she had no desire to tie Jonas to her with bonds of guilt. A proposal born of a sense of duty and moral obligation was not the way Tara wanted to start a marriage.

She wanted to be loved for herself. She needed a husband who wanted her first as a woman. Then as a friend. And lastly as a partner. Only then could he be the kind of father she wanted for her baby. A father who, like her own, showed by example what was really important in this world: true love, devotion to family and unerring trust in one's soul mate.

Wiping her mouth with a wad of toilet paper, Tara forced herself off the cold floor. However unpleasant it was going to be broaching the subject with her father, it was time to get on with the business of facing reality. Denial wouldn't change the fact that she was going to be a mother. Ready or not.

"Are you okay in there?"

The concern in Howard Summers's voice seeped under the bathroom door.

"I'm fine, Dad," she hastened to assure him. Worried about his health, she didn't want to upset him. Destroying the image of his perfect little girl just might be more than his heart could take.

The sound of the front doorbell ringing was welcome only because it postponed Tara's having to break the news to her father that he was going to become a grandfather.

"Let me get it," she told him, opening the bathroom door. "It sounds like the doorbell is stuck. I'll go see what's the matter."

"If it's a salesman, tell him we don't want any."

Tara padded to the front door in stocking feet to peer through the stained-glass panel. It was raining hard outside, which made it even more difficult to discern exactly who it was standing on the front stoop. She was reaching for the doorknob when she realized who it was. There, distorted in blurring stained-glass colors, stood Jonas, clutching something big and red to his chest.

Tara's heart lurched. God, but the very sight of him set her trembling. Wondering how he had tracked her down, she wheeled around and pressed her back against the door. She couldn't afford to let him see the effect he had on her. One look and he was bound to know that there was no real resistance here. That her hunger for him had consumed her night and day.

If she allowed herself to open that door, Tara knew she was likely to throw herself directly in his arms, forget her duty to her family altogether and blurt out that she was pregnant. Imagining the horror on his face at discovering he was going to be a father was enough to send that impulse flying out the window. Tara didn't want him to do the ''honorable'' thing by her. It wasn't fair to tie a maverick like him down for the rest of his life because of a baby he hadn't planned.

It wasn't fair to her to be married for the sake of a child alone.

Stubbornness and pride kept the door bolted between them.

Ten

"**G**o away!" Tara called out.

"What?" her father hollered from the other room.

"Nothing, Daddy. Nothing at all. Just some pesky salesman like you thought. I'll tell him we don't want anything he's peddling."

Pressing the doorbell again, Jonas refused to let up until Tara opened the heavy door a crack. Just enough to see raindrops spattering against the enormous bouquet of roses he held out to her.

"I said go away!" she hissed. "I don't want you upsetting my father. As you know, he's not well."

With that, she slammed the door shut before Jonas could get a single word out.

He lay on the doorbell again.

"What in hell is going on out there?" Howard Summers called out over the blare of the television in the living room. Hard of hearing, he had the set turned up full-blast. "Do you want me to come out there and shoo that pest away?"

"No, Daddy," Tara called back. "I've got everything under control."

It was a bold-faced lie. Her pulse was galloping like a runaway steed, her hands were shaking uncontrollably, and she thought she just might hyperventilate if she couldn't manage to get him to leave before her father came out to investigate what was going on for himself. Peering through the thick stained glass, she was horrified to discover that Jonas was actually beginning to draw a crowd.

"Please," she implored, opening the door only wide enough to let her words slip through. "Please go away! I'm no pity case, damn it!"

"No, but I am," Jonas replied, getting down on one knee in the rain.

"What you are is a jackass," she told him, shutting the door in his face again. Through the door she heard the initial lyrics to his loud off-key rendition of an old Carpenters' song that she'd confided back in Red Rock was a favorite of hers. Soaked to the skin and with equal determination, Jonas ignored the rain and the passersby who refused to pass by. Tara hoped if he finished his song without seeing her relent, he might give up and go away.

Pretending he wasn't there didn't work.

"Let him in. Let him in. Let him in!" the crowd gathering on the front lawn chanted.

Tara deeply resented their intrusion into her personal life. Had the old Victorian house not already been painted a lovely shade of pink, she was sure it would have blushed to have its dignity insulted so. Encouraged by the shouts of the gathering throng,

Jonas said, "I've been a fool searching the world over for the family I've never had only to discover that you are the only family I'll ever need, Tara."

At the mention of family, Tara's heart squeezed. He couldn't possibly understand the meaning of family and have spoken so hatefully to her the last time they had been together.

"Didn't you get my resignation?" she asked curtly.

"What in the name of God's good heaven is going on out there?" her father demanded, shuffling into the drawing room and wiping his eyeglasses on his robe.

He looked haggard and out of sorts. Seething at the thought of involving him in this whole sordid mess, Tara did her best to calm and distract him. The last thing he needed was to be sent into cardiac arrest again.

"It's nothing, Daddy. Why don't you go lie down for a bit and let me take care of this nut in my own way?"

It was just her luck that everyone seemed intent on ignoring her wishes today. Her father pulled back the lace curtain his wife had made especially to fit the tall parlor windows of the old Victorian home.

"Good Lord, girl. There's a veritable mob on our front lawn!" he exclaimed.

Luckily it was a small front yard.

"Maybe I should just call the police," Tara suggested in a panic, grabbing at anything that would prevent her father and Jonas from meeting face-to-face. Considering the way Howard Summers had reacted when he discovered how deeply Jonas had hurt her, Tara was as worried about her old employer's health as she was about her father's.

"Call the police?" he sputtered in disbelief. "Have

you forgotten I used to be on the force? As far as this household is concerned, I'm still the police!''

From his lacy vantage point he couldn't see Jonas well, only the sightseers enjoying the free entertainment from the sidewalk out front. Howard turned up his hearing aid in hopes of getting a better grasp of the situation.

"Good Lord, honey, some nitwit out there is singing his fool heart out. If you'll just get out of the way, I'll tell him to get lost. I don't like having our front porch treated as a sideshow.''

Thwarted in her attempts to keep her father from becoming involved, Tara grudgingly opened the door. Quickly Jonas stuck his foot over the threshold before the door could be slammed shut in his face again.

"I'm begging you, please just *go away!*" she pleaded.

"Not before I ask you something," he gasped. Singing in the rain was not nearly as easy as Gene Kelly had made it seem. His dark hair was plastered to his forehead, and he looked as if he had just been pulled from the bay.

The crowd went wild at the prospect of witnessing a full-fledged proposal.

"Say yes," called out a bystander sympathetic to Jonas's plight.

"Isn't this the most romantic thing you've ever seen?" whispered a pretty girl to her teenage escort.

Beneath a red-and-yellow umbrella, he squeezed her hand and impulsively called out, "Come on, lady. Say yes!"

A frowsy-looking matron, not so old that she couldn't remember being in love once herself, concurred. "If a man is willing to propose to you in the pouring rain in front of God and the whole world, he's worth forgiving.''

''He's not proposing, you idiots!'' Tara wanted to scream at them.

Of course, they couldn't know that Jonas was not, as he so eloquently put it himself, the marrying kind. If anything, Tara supposed in her absence he had discovered how difficult it had been to replace her. The only proposal she expected at the moment was the offer of a binding contract for her continued servitude. Taking care not to prick herself on the thorns, she took the beleaguered roses from Jonas's hands and hissed, ''All right, you can come in but only for a moment. My father has just been released from the hospital, and I don't want you upsetting him.''

''Say yes!'' the crowd chanted.

Tara glared at them. Jonas could have been a killer for all they knew. Nonetheless his actions made him their unlikely hero.

Grabbing him by one wet sleeve, Tara pulled Jonas inside. ''Show's over. Go home!'' she shouted before slamming the door on the dull roar of the crowd.

Disappointed that the performance was summarily concluded without the decided happy ending they so wanted to witness, the crowd dispersed.

Hatless, Jonas wiped an arm across his dripping face and surreptitiously eyed the coat rack in the corner.

''I hope you know it hasn't been easy tracking you down,'' he informed her.

''Poor baby,'' she muttered sarcastically.

Tara did not offer to take his coat or ask him to sit down, but kept him standing in the entryway like some unwanted solicitor.

"What do you want?" she demanded. "If it's a question about where something is filed back at the office, I'd be more than happy to help—without having to deal with you personally," she told him coldly.

At the mention of the word *office,* understanding lit Howard Summers's watery eyes. Looking at Jonas as if Satan had just crossed the threshold of his home, he puffed up in indignation. "So this is the boss you were telling me about, the one who treated you like a welcome mat. Just give me a minute to get my gun and I'll be right back."

"Daddy, don't..."

The note of panic in Tara's voice gave away her runaway emotions. She couldn't imagine anything more awful than having to act as a referee for the two men she loved most in the world.

"I'd really appreciate it if you'd just go into the other room and let me handle this myself," she told him.

Stepping out of the foyer and into the front room, Jonas bravely stuck out his hand. "Let me introduce myself, sir."

The older gentleman slapped the proffered hand out of the way. There was blood in his eye as he announced quite plainly, "I know who you are. You're the worthless SOB who broke my daughter's heart!"

Howard Summers's face was as red as the blossoms Tara held in her arms. Desperately trying to separate the two men, she stepped between them. Visions of her father clutching his chest and dying right in front of her flashed through her mind with frightful clarity. How Jonas managed a smile was something Tara could not comprehend. She wanted to slap it right off his handsome face.

When would that heart-wrenching desire go away? she wondered miserably.

"Actually I'm the *dumb* SOB who broke your daughter's heart," he corrected. "And I'm here to apologize abjectly for my stupidity for letting my fears blind me to the best thing that's ever come into my life. I love your daughter, Mr. Summers. If she would consider giving me a second chance, I'd like to spend the rest of my life trying to make myself worthy of her. I want to ask your blessing before I propose to her. You understand, of course, that whether or not you want me as a son-in-law won't deter me in the least."

As much as Tara clearly loved her father, Jonas had no intention of being dissuaded by him or anyone else, especially in matters of the heart. Life with his stepfather had taught him never to back down from a bully. Luckily he saw a sudden glint of approval in Howard Summers's eyes. Jonas recalled Tara saying that her grandfather had unsuccessfully tried to stand in the way of his daughter's marriage. Perhaps the old man was remembering a similar showdown many years ago.

"How am I supposed to know this isn't some clever act you're putting on just to get her back running your business smoothly for you?" he asked gruffly.

Tara's head was swimming. Worried she might faint, she dropped the bouquet of roses onto an end table, sank into a velvet armchair and tried to sort out her feelings. Everything was coming at her all at once. Considering that Jonas had yet to tell *her* directly that he loved her, she was in a state of shock. That he wasn't acting out of some misplaced sense of obli-

gation to give her baby a name and make up for the
mistakes of his own father was amazing. That Jonas
wanted her with or without an heir filled Tara with
the first real joy she'd felt since she'd packed her bags
and moved home.

Her heart overflowed with hope.

Her mind with doubt.

Placing her hands protectively over her stomach,
she wondered if it wasn't too much to expect Jonas
to exchange his traveling bags for all the extra baggage that came with a baby. A throbbing behind her
temples made it hard for Tara to think clearly.

On top of everything else she was appalled that
these two men were in the midst of haggling over her
as if she was some primitive tribal chattel. Had it ever
occurred to either of them that she might have a mind
of her own? How insulting to see that Jonas seemed
to think her acceptance of his forthcoming proposal
was automatic.

"Stop it!" she commanded.

The silence in the room was deafening as both her
father and Jonas turned to stare at her as if just realizing her presence.

"Don't you think it might be a good idea to ask
me before you propose to my father?" she asked
Jonas. "Although it does appear the two of you make
a lovely couple…"

"Now, honey—" her father began in a patronizing
voice that she recognized all too well from her childhood.

Jonas interrupted him in an equally patronizing
tone. "You're absolutely right."

Acting with the swiftness that had made him such
a successful entrepreneur, he again got down on one

knee in front of her chair. He took her hands tenderly into his. Having knelt in the rain for the better part of half an hour, he told himself he was willing to wear out the knees of his pants if necessary to prove his sincerity.

"I've been a fool to take your love for granted. To believe that just because my natural father couldn't love me that no one else could, either, especially someone as wonderful and lovely as you. These last weeks without you have been the longest and most miserable of my entire life. I've discovered that I'm not whole without you, sweetheart. Losing you means losing my soul. I love you with my entire being, and I would do anything in my power to make you the happiest woman on earth. Would you consent to marry me, Tara, and spend the rest of your life teaching me how to measure success in terms of the heart?"

Certain it was the most beautiful proposal ever uttered in the course of human history, Tara couldn't resist pushing a lock of his damp dark hair away from his forehead. How she loved that face! His eyes were so penetrating as he waited for her answer that she wouldn't have been much surprised if they discerned her closely guarded secret.

If love could be measured by a touch, Jonas thought, it would be in the way Tara ran her hands over his face. He closed his eyes as her fingertips hovered gently over the surface of his skin: along his jaw marked by a day's growth of stubble, the furrows of his forehead, the length of his nose, the curve of his lips, his eyebrows and finally his eyelids. She bent down and placed a kiss on his forehead.

Tara wondered why she was hesitating at all. Truly,

marriage to Jonas was the answer to all her prayers. She wanted nothing more than to be with him for the rest of her life. That he was willing to put aside his insecurities and propose to her in such a romantic fashion said a great deal for him. She was certain he would make a wonderful father. Their baby would have two loving parents and would never want for anything. There would be no need for Tara to work outside the home unless she wanted to. Financial considerations would never hold their child back.

She knew that Jonas would be hurt to discover she had set out to deceive him. In the dreamworld she was building around herself and this baby, never had she allowed herself to entertain thoughts of him someday finding out the truth. In light of the position in which Tara suddenly found herself, it was tempting to simply neglect mentioning her pregnancy until after the wedding. She could set the date as early as she wished. It had certainly been done before. The likelihood was she would have little trouble keeping it a secret. Surely hers wouldn't be the first "premature" baby ever born into the world.

Tara looked into Jonas's eyes and saw the love glistening there. She saw his certainty. And a future built on lies.

Taking a deep breath of air, she rendered a decision as irrevocable as the tiny life she was carrying.

"I'm sorry, Jonas, but I can't marry you."

Eleven

"**W**hy the hell not?"

It was her father's voice demanding a reason, but it was Jonas's eyes that pierced Tara's very soul. Behind a cloud of initial shock, the pain she glimpsed in their depths was very real. She hoped the damage to his only recently expressed vulnerability was not irreparable. Still, she had reason enough to do what she did. If her father would leave them alone for a while, she might even work up the courage to explain her actions to Jonas. Not that she had to, Tara reminded herself defensively.

"It had better not be because of some fool notion you have about needing to take care of me for the rest of my life. I may not be in the best of health, but I'm not an infant, and I refuse to be treated like one. I still have options, by God. Sacrificing your life for mine might not make a saint out of you, but I guarantee it would make a martyr out of me. Neither one of us wants or needs to live like that.''

Struck by the truth of his analysis, Tara nonetheless rushed to pacify him. "Taking care of you is a labor of love, Dad. You know you could never be a burden to me. I want you to please stop worrying that you're interfering in my life, because you're not.''

Jonas said nothing. He simply continued looking at her, questioning her with his eyes. Tara had hoped her refusal would send him indignantly out the front door, counting himself lucky for avoiding what might have been the biggest mistake of his life. Instead, she felt like a criminal. Angered that he could make her feel guilty without so much as saying a word, Tara wished he would just accept her answer and go on with his life unfettered by knowledge of his child and her great sorrow.

"What is it, then?" Jonas asked in a soft, yet cutting voice. "If it's not loyalty to your family, it must be me. How could you fall out of love with me so easily?"

Suddenly furious with his arrogance, she refused to be manipulated by the censure in his eyes. "Hasn't anyone ever told you *no* before?" Tara asked. "Did it ever occur to you to talk to me privately first before arriving on my doorstep and bringing the circus with you? Don't you think I might need to hear the words I love you before you ask my father for my hand in marriage like I'm some kind of child bride of a century ago, instead of a woman with a mind of my own? Have you ever considered the possibility that I might just have qualms about marrying you that aren't necessarily related to external problems with my family?"

Taking his cue from the slew of rhetorical questions leveled at Jonas like a machine gun, her father excused himself, hoping to get out of the line of fire intact. "I'll be in my bedroom if you need me," he told his daughter.

Though Tara had visions of him rifling through the closet for his old police-issue handgun, she let him go without any admonitions. As he had pointed out, he was not a child and she had no right to treat him so. It was a lesson she wished Jonas would learn in his interactions with her. As opposed to what he thought, she was not a young girl with nothing between her ears but a hope chest filled with the fluff of foolish dreams. The instant her father was out of the room, Tara shot yet another loaded question at Jonas.

"How dare you come in here acting like the injured party?" she demanded.

"This is a side of you I've never seen," Jonas said, shaking his head.

Tara couldn't decide if he was looking at her with newfound respect or trepidation. She didn't give him a chance to say that he found her fiery facets just as intriguing and appealing as the sweet disposition she usually saved for him. Instead, she railed against what she perceived to be an unfair judgment of her character.

"That's because I've been too busy trying to be exactly what I thought you wanted me to be. Your girl Friday. And Monday through Sunday, for that matter. Your best friend, loyal employee and sex kitten all rolled into one!"

The tiniest hint of a smile crinkled at the corners of Jonas's eyes. "Listen," he said in a soothing tone that did nothing whatsoever to calm her. "I don't blame you for being angry with me. I admit I've been a real jerk. Just remember that I'm new at expressing my feelings and that however long it takes, I'll wait for you to give me a second chance to prove myself to you."

"However long it takes?" she repeated incredulously.

Tara didn't have the luxury of unlimited time. Still, his offer was tempting. If she could just muster the courage to tell him about the baby, now was the perfect opportunity to let him prove whether he was a better man than his father—or give him the chance to back out gracefully before an innocent child was involved. Tara stared at him a long time, considering her options, then took a deep cleansing breath.

"I'd say about six months should do it."

Jonas looked at her as if she was speaking gibberish. When at last the significance of her words struck him with the force of a skyscraper toppling on him, he could do little more than mutter, "What?"

Still kneeling at her feet, he dropped his hand to Tara's stomach. His touch burned through the layers of her cotton shirt. That his caress could still be so utterly provocative made her silently curse her weakness as a woman. Rubbing a gentle circle over the snap of a pair of jeans that were just barely beginning to feel snug, Jonas's eyes grew wide with wonder.

"Do you mean to tell me that you're going to have our baby?" he asked in awe.

Pushing his hand angrily away, Tara tried to keep the quiver from her voice.

"No, *my* baby!" she corrected angrily. "Let me make it perfectly clear right here and now that I don't expect anything from you. Not so much as a dime of child support or even a perfunctory phone call on his or her birthday. I hereby absolve you of any guilt you may have over the conception of this baby. You're free to keep traveling the globe unencumbered, and you most certainly don't have to continue with this charade of a proposal out of some antiquated sense of moral obligation on my account.''

"You weren't even going to tell me, were you," he said, with a sudden grim set to his jaw. "You were so sure that I would react like my biological father and relinquish all rights to my own flesh and blood that you wouldn't even give me a chance to do the right thing!''

"The right thing,'' Tara stubbornly maintained, determined to let him walk away guilt-free with her heart as a bonus prize, ''is to let you get on with your life free of the very thing you despise most—a family. Whether you want to admit it or not, marriage and babies don't suit you. They're not exactly built to withstand the type of jungle adventures that thrill you.''

Her rationale cut like a scalpel. Whether he wanted the child or not, he was not about to walk away from his responsibilities. Good Lord, what kind of man did she think he was that he would prefer to remain in the dark about his own flesh and blood? For the first time in his life, Jonas found himself wondering whether his own mother had acted as presumptuously as Tara in keeping knowledge of his birth from his real father out of some misguided sense of protecting him. Such false nobility made him sick to his stomach.

Hurt turned to anger.

"A man has a right to know," he told Tara through a sudden blur of moisture.

As much as that shattered look on his face made her want to gather him into her arms, smother him with kisses and beg for his forgiveness, instead, Tara's voice trembled with rage.

"After the way you treated me when we got back from Red Rock, can you really blame me for not confiding in you? Wasn't I degraded enough without having to ask you to consider the welfare of a child you obviously didn't want? Or don't you remember swearing you didn't want children because your own childhood was so miserable and you were afraid of repeating the cycle?"

"Whatever I said, you have no right to deny me my children," Jonas said, allowing his voice to reflect his heart.

"Maybe not," Tara admitted grudgingly. For all her determination to remain strong, he was wearing her down. "For what it's worth I only just discovered that I'm pregnant. I'm sure sooner or later I would have gotten around to telling you."

"It's unfortunate that it had to be like this," he said, meaning it.

The knowledge that he wanted to be more than biologically involved in this baby's birth came as a great shock to Jonas. He was going to be a father! The knowledge filled his heart with a sense of wonder unlike anything he'd ever known before. Maybe he hadn't planned it, but he was determined to be the kind of father who contributed more than just his name and wages to the raising of his son or daughter. A daughter? The thought of having a baby girl was nothing short of terrifying. What he knew about little girls wouldn't fill a single sheet of a prescription note-pad. If she was anywhere near as beautiful as her mother, Jonas could plan on spending the next couple of decades fending off every boy in the vicinity.

All of a sudden he was planning a future not only for himself but for a family of three. Envisioning the perfect life for them was as easy as picturing the perfect wife. She was, after all, sitting right in front of him, looking even more beautiful than he remembered. And so high-spirited that he longed to tame her once again in his bed. He had never found pregnant women particularly appealing. This one, however, and the memory of how she had gone up in flames at his touch had his heart pounding and his blood running hot in his veins.

It was time to play the sympathy card. "My knees are getting sore," he told her. Never had he imagined that a proposal could be so agonizingly drawn out. "I'm asking again, Tara. Will you marry me?"

"And I told you before, you don't have to marry me because I'm pregnant."

"I know I don't *have* to!" he exploded. "How can I get it through your head that I *want* to?"

A warmth spread throughout Tara. It was impossible to rein in her hopes at this admission. Still, she wanted him to understand how much extra baggage would accompany her into any relationship they may forge.

"You know as well as I do that this isn't the best timing," she told him.

"Why not?" Jonas asked, recalling an old saying that if one waited until a person could afford a child, the world would be unpopulated.

Taking pity on him, she stood up and pulled him

to his feet, as well. A damp indentation of where he had knelt remained in the plush carpet, a visual reminder of his tenacity.

"On top of a baby coming before we've even had a chance to spend much time getting to know each other as a couple, I truly am tied down with my father, Jonas. Knowing how you stand on the issue, I have to tell that I'm truly honored by your proposal, but I still have reservations."

"But that was before," he protested hotly.

"Before what?"

"Before I actually met your father and discovered that I really like the cantankerous old bird. He's the kind of father I'm going to be. The kind who's going to protect our baby from big bad wolves like me."

His accompanying growl was predatory. It came from somewhere deep in this throat, and it sent shivers up and down Tara's arms. Putting his hands on her waist, he pulled her into his embrace and proceeded to trail hot kisses along her neck. She gasped in pleasure as he lingered at the hollow between her collarbones. Damn it. He knew how sensitive she was there.

"Besides," he crooned, "I have a funny feeling that my need for jungle adventures, as you so tactfully referred to them, will diminish as time goes by. What man needs exotic destinations, dangerous snakes, hordes of bloodthirsty mosquitoes and ridiculous government regulations when he could be snuggled up with the sweetest most wonderful wife in the world? And their beautiful baby."

Tears made it impossible for Tara to reply.

"I know I hurt your feelings, darling," he murmured. "Let me make it up to you."

Tara's willpower became all muddled. Her traitorous body was throbbing. Feeling the warmth of his breath just a heartbeat away, she asked in a throaty whisper, "And just how do you propose to do that?"

As his lips found hers, all resistance went away as a flood of raging desire rushed through her system. His kisses were warm and tender. Weak, she sank against him, and he tightened his grip. Emboldened, he grew more demanding, kissing her as if his life depended on it, his tongue seeking to claim her completely.

Tara gasped as he took her possessively by the hips and shifted his body so she could feel how hard she made him. She locked her arms around his neck to steady herself against the need coursing through her body. Her hips strained against his, rocking involuntarily in the age-old lovers' dance.

"I've missed you," he said, breathing heavily. It was, of course, a gross understatement. He'd almost died of wanting her.

"Don't punish me for being a fool," he implored. "I know I didn't treat you right, darling. I don't suppose it helps any to tell you that I was acting out of sheer terror. Nobody has ever made me feel the way you do, and I was afraid to open myself to those feelings. I couldn't stand the thought of ever being so vulnerable to another person. Now I understand that love isn't cautious or practical. That it isn't something that can be planned or orchestrated like a business deal. Love is saying, against all odds, I want to marry you and spend the rest of my life with you!"

Moved by his brave beautiful words, Tara quivered in his arms and forgave him with a kiss of her own. In it, she put every ounce of love overflowing the boundaries of her heart. *I love you,* it said, wordlessly capturing her emotions. Finally convinced of his sincerity and certain he was neither feeling coerced into marriage by a baby on the way nor resentful of including her family in their lives, she conveyed her happiness with a satisfied sigh. Overjoyed with the reality that the man of her dreams actually wanted her for herself and nothing else, Tara felt tears of joy run down her face.

She called out, ''You can put the gun away, Daddy. It looks like we're not going to need it for our wedding, after all!''

The next thing Jonas knew, Howard Summers was pumping his hand. ''Welcome to the family,'' the old man said, the twinkle back in his eye. ''Of course, you know if you ever do anything to hurt my daughter again, I won't hesitate to break your arm with a tire iron.''

''I appreciate the sentiment, sir,'' Jonas told him.

If it turned out that the child Tara was carrying was a girl, Jonas knew he would feel the same overwhelming need to protect her. He suspected it was a natural part of fatherhood. The special bond between a daddy and his little girl was a forever thing. Like marriage.

Looking at Tara, he felt his heart swell.

''I'd better do this while your father's still inclined to let me live,'' he said, drawing a velvet jewelry box from his coat pocket.

Inside was the most gorgeous ring Tara had ever seen: a two-carat marquis-cut diamond surrounded by glimmering emeralds, all of flawless quality. Personally she wouldn't have cared if it had been fashioned of gold foil. What it symbolized was of far more importance to her than any value a jeweler could place on it.

"It's beautiful," she whispered, slipping it onto her finger.

"You're beautiful," Jonas responded, looking deeply into a pair of eyes that sparkled more brightly than the jewels on her finger. Moist with emotion, they glistened with unshed tears of joy.

Truly Jonas had never seen anyone as incredibly lovely as this woman. She radiated that celebrated glow he'd always assumed was merely a condescending way to make pregnant women feel pretty despite their puffy ankles and ricocheting hormones. Jonas wasn't sure what the doctor would say about having sex in her condition, but now that he was convinced his father-in-law wasn't going to put a bullet in him, his body reacted with involuntary potency as Tara launched herself into his arms. The feel of her breasts pressed against his chest made him grow instantly needy.

"Good, that's settled then," Howard Summers proclaimed with a satisfied smile. "I'll be back in just a minute with something special to mark the occasion. Wait here."

Jonas hoped he took his sweet time. Since the moment Tara had answered the door in a pair of tight jeans that molded to her shape and a baggy yellow shirt designed to hide it, all he wanted to do was claim her as his own: legally, emotionally and physically. Not absence or time or the knowledge that she was pregnant with his child slaked Jonas's hunger for her. It was all he could do to refrain from finding the nearest bedroom and consummating their upcoming engagement before his father-in-law-to-be reappeared.

His eyes turned an even more intense shade of blue. He sought her mouth hungrily. She tasted like ambrosia would taste, Jonas imagined. He plundered the honeyed sweetness of her mouth for a long tender moment.

"Where's your bedroom?" he asked. Involuntarily his teeth chattered. Even his sexual fervor could not quell the damp chill settling into the very marrow of his bones.

Tara's eyes grew heavy-lidded. She whispered in his ear, "It's upstairs, but, Jonas, I hardly think it's advisable in my father's house to—"

Just then Howard Summers returned juggling a bottle of champagne and three glasses. He also had a calendar tucked under his elbow.

"I've been saving this champagne since the big millennium bash," Tara's father announced, full of cheerful goodwill for the young couple before him. "Figured if the world ended with all that Y2K crap the newscasters kept predicting, I might just as well go out with a bang!"

Whether it was bottles of champagne or shotguns, it seemed to Jonas that his father-in-law-to-be was big into all kinds of bangs. He was probably a real hoot on the Fourth of July. In any case, it seemed wise to humor the old man. Recalling the last toast he'd made—at the Double Crown Ranch to the health of his newfound family and the unfortunate incidents that had landed him in jail shortly thereafter—Jonas chose to let Howard make the salute.

"To the apple of my eye, my darling daughter, and to the man who'd better damn well make her happy," he said, raising his glass high in the air. "And to my grandchild on the way. May he or she be born healthy, be raised with love and patience and always be treated as a special gift from heaven above.''

Feeling the world shift like sand beneath her feet, Tara gasped. "How did you know, Daddy?"

"I can put two and two together as well as the next guy. And I eavesdropped on your conversation from the other room," he admitted with a wink.

Tara was happy that the engagement ring on her finger served to offset any disappointment her father might be feeling about her lack of premarital restraint.

The clinking of their three glasses together symbolized the joining of families. This gracious old house was far from the lavish surroundings of the Fortune family, but Jonas already felt at home here. Her father may be gruff and a little rough around the edges, but his feelings for his daughter were sincere. He couldn't help but like the old curmudgeon.

Jonas imagined how spoiled their child would be growing up in the midst of a real family, the likes of which he himself had never known. Picturing in his mind a little girl with eyes the exact same color as her mother's sliding down that grand old banister in a race with her numerous cousins made him smile in anticipation of good times to come. Doting grandparents and aunts and uncles should spoil every child in such a manner, a way that left all children feeling secure and adventurous and loved regardless of their circumstances.

Even to a connoisseur such as himself, the cheap champagne tasted better than any Jonas had ever sampled. Howard poured himself and his soon-to-be son-in-law another glassful. Thinking of the baby, Tara declined any more than an obligatory sip to salute their upcoming wedding. Without further ado, her father proceeded to open the calendar and spread it out on the dining-room table.

"Just as soon as we pencil in a date, I'll call your brothers to tell them the good news."

"The sooner the better," Jonas suggested.

Fearing Tara might change her mind, he was as eager to solidify a date as her father seemed to be. Not to mention that if he had to wait much longer to satisfy his sexual appetite, he was likely to explode with longing.

Getting the impression that both her father and her fiancé were once again planning her life without her, Tara put her foot down. A thunderous expression clouded her face.

"If anyone cares to hear what I have to say on the subject, there is one little condition that I want met before you both get back to planning my wedding."

Hope shone in her eyes as she focused her attention on Jonas. "Weddings are about families. If we're going to get married, it's important that both our families come together. I want you to call your aunt Miranda and ask your side of the family to our wedding."

"*If* we're going get married?" Jonas parroted in disbelief. "I thought it was all settled."

Her request was completely unacceptable. Why would he want to ruin the happiest day of his life with the unwanted presence of a family who had caused him nothing but trouble? He'd just as soon ask the devil and his cohorts to accompany them on their honeymoon.

Tara worried that he was right. After all, a long time had passed since that surprise announcement and not another word had been heard on the subject.

"I want to invite them nonetheless," she said with a determined lift of her chin.

Jonas softened. He was not about to lose her now over something as trivial as the wedding-guest list. Besides, he was certain the Fortunes would snub the invitation, anyway, and put an end to this nonsense. And as long as there was no real risk involved, he saw no reason not to concede.

"Maybe we can work something out, since you seem to have your heart set on my not only fitting in with your family but my own, as well. I did receive a letter the other day from the Fortunes' law firm summoning me to San Antonio. I was going to ignore it, but if you'd be willing to come along as my wife, I just might be persuaded to start our honeymoon along the scenic River Walk that city is so proud of. But the instant I'm formally 'disinherited' and you're convinced that pursuing a relationship with the Fortunes is a lost cause, I want to fly you to a very special tropical destination very few people even know about. Just promise me you won't be too disappointed in what the lawyer has to say and you'll try to accept that my family is never going to be as close as yours. I don't mean to seem inflexible, but I do believe it's better not to subject our child to the kind of dysfunctional behavior excess wealth and notoriety brings."

Although no authority on the subject, Jonas was convinced that the best way to raise a child was to do more with them and give them less. He wanted to spare their child exposure to any questionable influences for as long as he possibly could.

Tara met his gaze unflinchingly. "I'll promise you—if you'll promise me to hear the lawyer out. And if the news isn't as bad as you're predicting, that you'll consider spending the entire honeymoon in Texas getting to know your family." She corrected herself. "Getting to know our baby's family, that is."

"You've got to be kidding!" Jonas exclaimed in genuine disbelief. "You'd rather honeymoon in Texas than on one of the most exotic secluded islands in the world?"

Tara ran a hand over the strong curve of a jaw both stubborn and strong. "I'd just want to give the Fortunes a chance to prove themselves on their own merits and not stereotype them as rich socialites out to bend you to their wishes. They have a lot more to offer than just money, you know."

Though the hard glint in Jonas's eyes softened some, it did not fade completely. "I suppose you're one of those bleeding hearts who buys into that whole 'it takes a village to raise a child' philosophy?"

"Absolutely. Dad always told us kids that you don't just marry the person you fall in love with, you marry the whole family."

The thought of marrying Tara's entire clan was more intimidating than Jonas wanted to admit. Still, short of becoming a punching bag for her brothers, he would die trying to fit into this tightly knit family. If that meant he had to schedule his wedding around his father-in-law-to-be's idiosyncrasies and his bride's idealistic plans to mend his broken family ties, then so be it.

Switching his attention to Howard Summers, Jonas told him. "Anytime, anyplace, any guest list, any type of ceremony your daughter wants is just fine with me.

Whatever makes Tara happy will make me happy. All I'd really like from you, sir, is your blessing.''

The older man stuck out his hand, and despite his health problems, his grip was strong. ''You've got it, son.''

The faith placed in that handshake made Jonas want more than anything else in this world to live up to this man's expectations. Notwithstanding the cold reception he'd initially gotten, Jonas wanted Howard's respect. It struck him as serendipitous that his marriage might well provide him with the kind of father he'd always longed for.

At the sight of the two men she loved most clasped in a handshake that could only be described as sacred, Tara had to fight back tears.

Then her father turned to her and scolded good-naturedly, ''If you don't let the poor man get a change of clothes, he may well die of pneumonia before you can get him to the altar.''

Grateful somebody had finally noticed his discomfort, Jonas grabbed the proffered sympathy and ran with it. ''I really would like to get out of these wet things,'' he said, hoping Howard would understand that he wanted some time alone with his daughter.

And get your daughter out of her clothes, too, he was tempted to add, but recalling the earlier tire-iron threat, thought better of it.

''Then I'd like to take you out for a nice dinner to celebrate,'' he told Tara.

She nodded in agreement. ''Just let me call one of my brothers to come stay the night with Dad. Then I'll pack a few things, and you can take a hot shower back at your place. I really don't want you to catch a cold before the wedding.''

Before they left, Jonas told Howard to "pick any date you want and just let us know what works best for you and your sons."

Clearly he would have been just as happy skipping the San Antonio rendezvous with the Fortunes altogether and heading straight to the justice of the peace. Or better yet to the closest motel.

Tara's smoldering gaze wordlessly confirmed that she was thinking along similar lines. "Don't wait up," she told her father as she left to gather up a few things for the evening.

He was already on the phone and deep into conversation by the time Jonas and Tara pulled out of the driveway. Far more hungry for her lover's touch than for food, Tara found herself resenting the expensive bucket seats in the Jaguar that Jonas handled with such ease. Rather than snuggling up against him, she settled for draping one hand on his shoulder and caressing his neck. She toyed with his earlobe and was gratified when she coaxed a satisfied sigh from him.

"If you don't watch what you're doing, I'm going to pull over to the side of the road and let nature take its course."

"If *you* don't watch what *you're* doing, we're going to end up spending our honeymoon in the hospital," Tara teased, reminding him to keep his eyes on the road.

Her diamond flashed in the glow of oncoming headlights, scattering myriad tiny prisms across the ceiling of the vehicle. The ring on her finger emboldened her to drop her hand to Jonas's lap and test her womanly powers on him. His involuntary reaction exhilarated her as he punched the gas pedal hard.

* * *

A little over an hour later, they arrived at Jonas's posh condominium in record time without a ticket for speeding. Tara wrinkled her nose in distaste at the decidedly stylish decor. Thanks to a chic decorator and an efficient housekeeper, no one would even guess somebody actually lived here. Not so much as an old pair of sneakers was out of place in the sleek but cold surroundings.

Wavering between chills from being in wet clothes far too long and flashes of heat at the thought of finally being alone with the woman he loved, Jonas draped his damp coat over the back of a chair.

"Why don't you make yourself comfortable while I get changed?" he suggested, heading for a long hot shower.

San Francisco's skyline glittered in the darkening evening haze like some enchanted fairy kingdom. Tara was far less interested in the spectacular view from the living-room window than she was in a more intimate show involving one virile male stripping for her benefit alone.

"I've got a better idea," she said, her voice husky and warm as whiskey. "Why don't I make you comfortable and help you change?"

Jonas stopped in his tracks. His eyes darkened with yearning.

"Aren't you hungry?" he asked, wanting to make sure he hadn't somehow misunderstood her motives.

After the evening's dramatic performance, Jonas wasn't about to risk offending her now. While lovemaking was very important to him, he also understood that a woman liked to be romanced. He also suspected that Tara might well feel shortchanged in that department. Having promised her dinner and a night to celebrate their engagement, he wanted to make the evening one to remember.

So did she.

"Ravenous," Tara assured him, stepping forward to help him disrobe.

Her hands grasped the hem of his cream-colored cable-knit sweater and pulled it over his head in one swift motion. Beneath the sweater a damp shirt clung to skin that made her think of bronze satin. Tara didn't fumble as she proceeded to unbutton the shirt and run her hands across his broad chest. Jonas shrugged off the shirt impatiently and reached for the fly of his jeans. She brushed his hand away.

"Let me," she commanded gently.

"My pleasure," Jonas groaned in reply, wondering how he was ever going to find the patience to endure such heavenly torture.

The state of his arousal was made more and more obvious with the undoing of each brass button. Cupping him with one hand, Tara pushed his jeans down to his knees with the other. She felt a heady sense of female dominance as she sat him down on his black leather couch to remove his shoes. They were still sopping wet, as were the socks, which she tossed out of the way without regard to where they fell.

A moment later his briefs went in the same direction.

"Come here," Jonas said, a shiver of anticipation running through his naked body.

"Whatever date we finally settle on, I really don't want to take any chances that you'll be sick for the wedding. First a shower to warm you up. I'll join you if you like," Tara cooed.

Jonas didn't have to be asked twice. Taking her by

the hand, he led her to the luxurious bathroom adjoining his bedroom. She barely had a chance to glance at the king-size bed and darkly masculine comforter before he had the water running at full blast.

"Time for me to return the favor," he murmured in her ear. Jonas wasn't sure who this brazen woman was who'd switched places with his modest bride-to-be, but he was determined to encourage her in every way possible.

His patience stretched thin, he hastened to remove Tara's clothes without ripping them. First came the oversize sweatshirt, then the sexy camisole. Jonas admired the matching bra spilling over with creamy white flesh. Pregnancy had rounded Tara's figure, making it even more voluptuous than he remembered. The exposed cleavage was a beautiful sight to behold. Releasing her breasts from bondage, Jonas gently cupped them both in his hands.

Tara shuddered with delight as he bent down to suckle. Taunting, teasing, encircling, his tongue was a magical tool as he took her intimately in his mouth and made the act a prayer. She did not know when he managed to strip her of her pants, but suddenly, standing before him naked, Tara felt self-conscious.

Jonas ran his hands across her still-flat tummy and wondered aloud how she could hide the secret of a child within. "I promise to be gentle tonight," he assured her. "I wouldn't want to hurt it."

Tara smiled as she corrected him. "*It* is a baby. And according to my reading on the subject, he or she is far too tiny as of yet to be bothered at all by our making love. It may be a concern later in the pregnancy, but as long as we're careful, I doubt it."

"Good," was all Jonas managed to rasp out before

Tara took him firmly in hand and led him into the shower stall.

All thought of making her a doctor's appointment first thing in the morning disappeared. Jonas had no idea that she could be such an unmitigated tease. His only memories of her had been of sweet innocence and an eagerness to please. This was the woman who had taught him the difference between making love and having meaningless sex. Knowing he was utterly ruined for other women, he was thrilled to discover that his wife-to-be had another side to her personality: a playful bewitching side that seemed to know just how to bring him to the brink of his self-control, then step back out of the way and leave him gasping for more.

"'Tis a dangerous game you're playing, vixen," he informed her as hot water beat down to envelop them in a steamy cloud that coaxed the chill from his bones.

With a throaty giggle Tara grabbed a bar of soap and began lathering him all over. The shower was roomy enough to accommodate them both comfortably. Jonas returned the courtesy. Flesh made slippery and supple with soapy suds begged for immediate gratification, but again Tara implored Jonas to wait just a little longer.

Turning him around to face the showerhead, she poured shampoo into the palm of her hand and began working it into his thick thatch of dark hair. Her massage of his scalp brought another moan of pleasure from him. As did the act of slipping up behind him and curling her body around his. Cradled in this intimate spoonlike position, she rubbed the front of her body against the back of his.

Jonas hurried to rinse the shampoo from his hair, then turned to take her in his arms. Leaning her head against his shoulder, Tara let the soothing water wash away any doubt she may have ever had about whether this man truly loved her. Without prior knowledge of the baby she was carrying, he had sought her out and subjected himself to public humiliation on her behalf. She smiled at the memory of him belting out that song on bended knee in the pouring rain. He was also willing to accept her rowdy family as part of the package, and even more amazingly, to seek his own out once again at her request. Best of all, he seemed genuinely happy about the baby their love had produced.

Life couldn't get any better.

Filled with a sense of joy and abundance, Tara wanted to give Jonas all of her: heart, mind and body. She vowed to hold nothing back.

So when he muttered in agony, ''I can't wait a second longer,'' she reached behind him and turned the faucet off.

I love you, she wrote in the condensed moisture on the shower door before opening it and letting the steam escape into the bathroom itself. Jonas stopped only long enough to punctuate the statement with a heart before stepping out himself.

Tara was waiting there to present him with a huge fluffy towel. She proceeded to rub Jonas down from top to bottom and back up again for good measure, stopping wickedly to pause at his most erogenous zones along the way. Wet tendrils of blond hair clung to Tara's back. Slicked away from her face, it left her utterly exposed to this man's scrutiny.

Wrapping a clean towel around her, Jonas picked her up and carried her into his bedroom. Tara linked her arms around his neck and held on for the ride of her life. Laying her on the bed as gently as a china doll rather than a woman of aching flesh and hot blood, Jonas paused an excruciating moment to drink in the sight of her. She tried not to squirm beneath his gaze. His arousal, so utterly magnificent, made her feel powerful yet ever so vulnerable.

She opened herself to him, and he groaned at the invitation, tumbling wordlessly onto the bed beside her.

That God intended the joining of flesh to be a sacred act was a certainty in Tara's mind as Jonas entered her. Both were already worked into such a state of frenzied need that neither was aware of anything but the sensation of each other's unique taste, scent and touch. Nothing else in the world mattered. Shuddering in his arms, Tara writhed beneath him, reaching her peak almost instantly. With a startled moan, she gathered him close, murmuring incoherent endearments. Jonas exploded, emptying himself into the warm womanly vessel, behind which, unbelievably, his child was safely growing.

That such an act had already resulted in the conception of a child was of too miraculous a nature to take for granted. Rolling into the crook of his arm, she snuggled against him.

"I love you," she whispered sleepily.

"I'll love you forever," he promised, vowing to tell her that every single day for the rest of his life.

Slick with sweat, spent and satiated, he wrapped his body around Tara and welcomed her as his soul mate for eternity. Propping himself on an elbow, he luxuriated in studying her. Her hair was spread about her like a shimmering halo. As if to reassure himself that she was indeed real, Jonas brushed his fingertips over the contours of her face. Eyes still glazed with passion regarded him with unconcealed love. To be thus entrusted with a person's heart was serious business, and Jonas was determined never to let her down again.

As she drifted off to sleep oblivious to the sparkling lights reflecting off the ocean, curled against her lover as snugly as a butterfly in its cocoon, Tara placed his hand over her tummy.

"We both adore you," she told Jonas, speaking for the baby conceived by their passion.

"You both need some sleep," he responded, his voice hoarse with emotion in the darkened room.

Long after hearing Tara's breath deepen into sleep, Jonas stayed awake plotting, scheming and simply reveling in the feel of his wife-to-be's beautiful body. Having found his family at last, he vowed to do everything in his power to keep them safe forever. He prayed that the Fortunes would not attempt to do anything to undermine his efforts.

Like trying to manipulate his child as his stepfather had him.

Or turning Tara against him again.

Thirteen

If Jonas was surprised later in the week by Miranda's gleeful acceptance of his wedding invitation over the phone, he was totally flabbergasted when she suggested they actually have their wedding at the Double Crown Ranch. *Horrified* was a better word. Had Tara not been on the extension, he would have turned his scheming aunt down flat. As it was, Tara was so thrilled with the idea that he didn't dare disappoint her. Recalling that her only stipulation regarding their wedding was that both families come together, Jonas wasn't about to jeopardize a lifetime of happiness over any qualms he might have about his relatives.

And so it was that Jonas found himself on a plane headed to Texas to plan his wedding at the very place where he had been arrested for attempted murder. If that didn't prove his love to Tara, he didn't know what could.

He wished there was some way to shake himself of the feeling that something of monumental consequence awaited him in Texas. Something that didn't include another set of handcuffs.

Having never traveled first-class before, Tara luxuriated in the extra leg room and the attention lavished on them by the stewardess. She had a window seat, and she loved the bird's-eye view of the world. Leaving the ocean and the rolling green panorama of California behind and heading toward the dusty plains of the Southwest made her feel like a modern-day pioneer, traveling the Oregon Trail in reverse. She couldn't help but hope that Texas would be their own special promised land. A place where they could stake out a homestead of the heart.

Tara knew her family would accept Jonas on his own merits, both as a husband and a father. Still, no matter how warmly her relations affirmed him, it wasn't the same as being a part of one's own genetic family. As much as Jonas protested to the contrary, she felt that he was masking a deep abiding hurt. A hurt she feared would tear not only at his soul but also at the very fabric of their marriage and perhaps emotionally distance him from the child she was carrying.

Though she hadn't dared to voice it, Tara understood that a failure to reconcile with the Fortunes could very well put a halt to their wedding plans. She had no intention of marrying half a man. Her hand instinctively reached out for her stomach, rubbing it covertly and reassuring the baby that she would do everything in her power to help Jonas trust in his intuitive heart. To follow that little voice locked deep inside him telling him to find his family—and to forgive them.

Not that Tara was without doubts, either. If she let herself, she could easily become worried sick wondering if she had made the right choice in urging him to return to Texas. There was a definite possibility that the lawyers could well confirm every ugly suspicion that Jonas had about his relations and crush any chance of family harmony for good.

Still, as a woman and a creative spirit, Tara felt more comfortable than Jonas following her heart's urges. Call it intuition, a gut feeling or simply wishful thinking, she felt driven to remove any obstacle keeping her future husband from feeling complete. She understood his worry about the Fortunes' influence on their unborn baby, but thought his concerns groundless.

She smiled. Why, the way Jonas talked, the Fortunes were as dangerous as the Mafia in their desire to control others. From her chance meeting with Miranda, Tara remained unconvinced. She couldn't imagine such a warm lovely woman as a villain. Jonas had been quick to point out that since his dear aunt had run off at the tender age of seventeen to become an actress, Tara shouldn't be so easily deceived by her performance. She suspected that Jonas's fears were more grounded in the pain of being arrested for a heinous crime than from any "truth" he had discovered about his relatives.

Both Tara and Jonas were startled to hear the pilot's announcement that they were almost at their destination.

"Isn't that the San Antonio River?" Tara asked, looking out the window.

Her smile reached into Jonas's very being and filled him with a sense of undeserved joy. Other than opening his dusty heart up to her, what had he done to deserve such an angel?

"I believe so."

No wider than a country lane, the river was green in color, languidly snaking through the heart of Texas's oldest city. Though Jonas had no interest in the river, he leaned across Tara's seat to humor her. Just brushing against her body was enough to make him glad he did. He kissed her gently, reveling in the salty taste of airline peanuts lingering on her lips. Jonas could never get enough of those sweet sweet kisses. Unlike his experience with other women, in which kissing was an art perfected merely to hasten the act of intercourse, kissing Tara was pleasure in itself. One chaste kiss in public and his body immediately hardened with longing.

"Have you ever heard of the Mile High Club?" he asked, nuzzling her neck before returning to an upright position in his own seat.

The twinkle in her soft brown eyes assured him that indeed she had. Squeezing his hand, she informed him in a provocative voice, "I'm not a member as of yet. I do hope you're willing to remedy that as soon as possible."

Looking around at the full first-class section, Jonas ground his teeth in frustration. "Even if it means having to buy my own plane!"

"Business is good," Tara assured him, "but it's not that good. Need I remind you we have our baby's college education to think of?"

She didn't doubt for a second that Jonas was capable of buying and piloting his own aircraft, or submarine, for that matter. Whatever he wanted, he got sooner or later. She prayed that whatever fate awaited them on the ground would never get in the way of their wanting each other. Squeezing her eyes shut and grabbing hold of Jonas's hand as if it were a brake, Tara braced herself for a bumpy landing. She took it as a good sign that, despite her expectations, the landing actually ended up uneventful. Tara just hoped the visit with the lawyers tomorrow and with her soon-to-be in-laws later the following day would go off half as smoothly.

It didn't take them long to flag down a taxi. Jonas had made reservations in a posh hotel within walking distance of San Antonio's Paseo del Rio—the famous River Walk that celebrated the city's special heritage and beauty. After duly "breaking in" the honeymoon suite, they dressed and headed for the River Walk, where an array of pungent smells and colorful sights awaited them. Famished from a leisurely afternoon of making passionate tender love, they perused the menus posted outside the many cafés lining the walkway. They finally succumbed to the Tex-Mex aroma of a restaurant with red-and-white umbrellas flagging their outdoor tables. Gorging on a huge platter of spicy fajitas for two and generous margaritas—hers minus any alcohol for the sake of the baby—they shared a single serving of caramel flan for dessert.

Then, as they strolled hand in hand along the winding walkway, they admired the unique blend of cultural wares displayed along the banks of the deceptively peaceful river. Unusually warm mid-November weather in San Antonio made more than a jacket unnecessary. Tara wore a shawl over a gauzy dress that swirled loosely around her body. The flowing style of her dress deemphasized the barely perceptible bulge of pregnancy, but did nothing to hide the full swell of her breasts.

Remembering the feel of those soft mounds in his hands, Jonas hated to see her don a shawl and deprive him of the sight of those delectable curves. Reminding himself that their hotel was just around the corner, Jonas reined in his lust and indulged his bride-to-be in some sidewalk shopping.

They were not the only lovers wandering along the promenade. Passersby in all types of garb ranging from cowboy hats to jogging sets to three-piece suits lingered beneath the awning of trees. Music floated out of swinging doors of a cantina. Seized by a sudden romantic impulse, Jonas pulled Tara into his arms.

A Mexican mariachi band serenaded the young lovers as they danced beneath the canopy of stars just beginning to light the evening sky. Swaying to the music with her arms wrapped around Jonas's broad shoulders, Tara felt completely happy with their baby cushioned between them. Jonas's hands roamed possessively over her body, and she felt no compunction to remove them.

Like the food they had consumed, Jonas's scent was spicy enough to make Tara feel flushed. Breathing deeply, she reveled in the sheer sensuousness of the moment. One hand fondled the fabric of the shirt he wore while the other caressed the strong line of his jaw. And when he kissed her, she felt herself spinning wonderfully out of control like one of the funny handcrafted marionettes she'd purchased at one of the open-air booths they'd stopped at along the way.

"Let's take a boat ride," she suggested impetuously, gesturing at the barges on the river.

Jonas agreed. Ever cautious, he made sure Tara wasn't jostled unnecessarily as she took her seat on one of them. "This could just as easily have been a gondola in Venice," he said ruefully, still fretting that she had been shortchanged in the honeymoon department.

All in the pursuit of a lost cause to reunite him with a family that once considered him capable of murder.

Tara didn't see it that way at all. Her eyes were aglow with excitement as they pushed off and began their gentle journey down the river. Cuddling up against Jonas's chest and drawing his arms around her, she hastened to reassure him, "I couldn't be any happier than I am right now with you. I was hoping you'd come to understand that true contentment isn't tied to a place. It's something you carry with you from place to place with the one you love."

Dropping a kiss atop her blond head, Jonas considered the profusion of stars overhead. "How did I get so lucky to have found someone so sexy *and* so smart?"

It was a sentiment he repeated over and over again as they made their way under picturesque arched bridges through the very soul of San Antonio and eventually back to their luxurious hotel to test his stamina once again....

The following morning they stumbled out of the law offices of Finch and Foresman, blinking in the bright sunlight. Tucked in Jonas's pocket was a copy of the document he had just signed. Considering the weightiness of its contents, it was relatively short in legalese.

The sum of ten million dollars to be transferred to the personal account of one Jonas Goodfellow Fortune at the date specified below...

Though both Miranda and Ryan had specifically told their nephew about his inheritance, Jonas hadn't believed it would ever really materialize. Utterly dazed at the reality of becoming a multimillionaire overnight, he would have walked straight into traffic had not Tara reached for his hand to stop him.

Assured by the lawyer that there were no strings attached, Jonas was struggling with the fact that it was strictly a gift. "To make up for any pain and distress caused by your father, Cameron Fortune," were the lawyer's exact words.

Jonas was in a state of shock.

Tara was in a state of elation.

Not because she was about to marry a very wealthy man, but because this proved once and for all that Jonas had been wrong about his relatives. Contrary to his expectations, they had neither sought to cut him off from his inheritance nor to control him through it. Without any accompanying fanfare or thought of personal loss, they had simply handed him his birthright and invited him home.

Tara held her tongue, deciding it best to give him time to absorb the shocking news in his own way. Reality was taking a while to sink in. Clearly Jonas was having a hard time accepting events that would force him to change the way he viewed his world. Initially he had resisted the idea entirely, thinking it too farfetched to be believable. Now, though still leery of any attempts at controlling him or, God forbid, his children through that money, he was gradually coming to grips with the idea that the Fortunes were not cut from the same shabby cloth he had once believed. Those dark impressions had been cemented during his incarceration while contemplating a life behind bars, framed for a crime he did not commit.

Of course when he considered the circumstantial evidence objectively, he had to admit that all the signs had indeed pointed to him. Had he been the one poisoned and languishing in a hospital bed, he supposed he might have jumped to a similar conclusion as Ryan Fortune had—that the guest who'd brought the wine was likely the same person who'd tampered with it.

They walked aimlessly for several city blocks until they found themselves standing in front of the Alamo, along with just about every other tourist in the city. Stepping inside where it was cool, Tara felt goose bumps rise along the length of her arms. It was a spooky place, one that evoked the fear and desperation of dying men who refused to admit defeat. Jonas, too, felt spirits moving next to them as he fingered the bullet holes in the thick fortress walls.

"I think Texans have the right idea," he said unexpectedly.

"What do you mean?" Tara whispered out of reverence for the dead.

"Here's a place where brave men gave up their lives rather than surrender in spite of overwhelming odds. Though it was a tragic military defeat, Texans turned that loss into a rallying cry. Rather than burying their failures, they take inspiration from them and make monuments out of them."

Keeping his own voice low, he continued on with his train of thought. "There's a lesson here. I think

Fourteen

"**I**'ve always wanted to buy a piece of property with a stream on it," Jonas confided as they drove along the back roads to Red Rock, dreaming of lazy days spent with children of his own, casting flies and hopes over rippled water. Jonas could barely remember a time when he hadn't been beleaguered by the demands of crushing traffic, the beep of a pager, the ring of a phone or the needs of a company that consumed his heart and soul.

Tara was glad to see the Texas hill country work its magic on the hard-boiled urban man who once upon a time would have scoffed at the very thought of leaving the city. As much as she, too, loved the ocean, the culture and the hustle and bustle of San Francisco, thoughts of a gentler less-harried lifestyle had begun to appeal to her far more now that she was going to be a mother.

The Fortune roots were sunk deep in this soil, their heritage vested in each breathtaking vista. Even for a stranger to these parts, this land had a strong pull. Close enough to San Antonio to provide a city's full cultural diversions, the Double Crown Ranch was also far enough away to allow real serenity to penetrate the layers of pretense that so often accompanied great wealth and fame.

A man could be himself here, Jonas suspected, without anyone paying him too much fuss. For someone who'd had to grovel for ice-cream money as a kid, it was hard for him to comprehend that whatever he wanted monetarily was in his grasp now, thanks to the family he'd foresworn almost immediately upon discovering their existence. Working hard for a living was so ingrained in his personality that he wasn't quite sure who he'd be without a job. The idea of having more than enough for the rest of his life without ever having to worry about paying the bills again was quite simply beyond him.

"What do you suggest we do with all that money we have?" he asked Tara.

Her laughter was like the sound of chimes tinkling in a gentle breeze. "For starters," she said, leaning across the seat to kiss his cheek. "You could use it to give yourself enough time off to figure out who you are. To separate yourself from your job."

Indeed, Jonas had defined himself by his career for so long that the very thought rocked him to the core of his being.

Testing his earlobe between her teeth, Tara told him, "It will give you a chance to get used to fatherhood, too, and to get to know your family. The one that made everything possible. As you're about to find out when you have a child of your own, family is the most important thing in this world.''

The thought of populating a *real* home with a noisy joyful brood of their own opened Jonas's heart to the possibility of living life with them, rather than his job, at its center.

''Just remember that building a house with unlimited money at our disposal is far less important than providing our children with a secure happy environment,'' she explained. ''I'm thinking less in terms of fancy gated estates and more in the line of the kind of house I was raised in, only a little bigger. I think it's important for a child to have his own room, don't you? A place with banisters to slide down and a big yard with lots of trees for climbing and enough space for a couple of dogs to have room to run without bothering the neighbors.''

Jonas thought looking at Tara's face was like staring at the sun. She glowed with excitement as she made plans for their future.

''And the same sense of security and love you had growing up,'' he added, thinking back to the cold tomb where he'd been raised. There was no bitterness in his words, only a sad finality. ''I want that, too, baby. More than you can possibly know.''

Even though Tara had been the one pushing so hard for this reunion, she felt herself becoming increasingly tense as they neared their destination. Just because she had been right about his inheritance did not necessarily mean his relatives would not want to manage their lives as Jonas feared. She hoped they understood she would fight like a bear to keep anyone from trying to mold their child into anything other than his or her unique self. Hoping Jonas wouldn't realize how nervous she was, Tara kept up a steady uncharacteristic chatter that was far more telling than silence ever would have been. Jonas squeezed her hand reassuringly as they turned the final bend in the road. Her words stopped in midsentence as she got her first look at the famous Double Crown Ranch. The massive gateway made it impossible to mistake this ranch for any other.

The estate was far grander than anything Tara had ever imagined. Miles and miles of fence stretching out on either side of the car marked Fortune territory for all to see and put her in mind of historic plantations. It appeared that her soon-to-be in-laws owned half the state of Texas.

"I had no idea," Tara squeaked, painfully aware of how out of place she might look in her comfy suede boots and the bright Mexican skirt she'd bought off the streets of San Antonio on a whim.

The largest of the several houses on the estate belonged to Ryan. The huge Spanish-style hacienda sat at the end of an extensive driveway as picture-perfect as a postcard. Horses grazing in idyllic pastures lent country charm to the scene. The closer they got to the main house, the larger it loomed. Tara wondered if poor Cinderella had ever considered bolting from the carriage before being dropped off on the castle doorstep.

Her fears and trepidation melted away the instant she saw Miranda step onto the veranda and throw open her arms in welcome. In some unfathomable way Tara felt as if she was coming home to her own mother. It wasn't so much that Miranda shared any physical similarities with her deceased mother. Other than an upswept Grace Kelly hairstyle, they were, in fact, very different in coloring and carriage. Rather, it was the sense that this gracious woman exuded warmth and an acceptance of others that made Tara feel cherished and loved.

As Miranda stepped off the porch, hastening to meet them halfway between the car and the porch, a gentle breeze caught the soft silken layers of the dress she wore. The colors of the rainbow billowed around her shapely figure, reminding Tara for all the world of a fairy godmother come to greet them. The kiss she bestowed on Tara's cheek seemed as natural as if they had known each other for years and years.

"I'm so glad you decided to come," she told them both, giving Jonas a similar enthusiastic welcome. "Don't you think this will be a lovely spot for your wedding?"

Tara said she couldn't think of a lovelier spot in all the world.

"Don't worry," Miranda assured her. "I'll only give you as much help as you want. I promise not to run all over you."

Tara's eyes teared up. Since her own mother was dead, she couldn't think of anything nicer than having this marvelous woman step in and help her plan the most important day of her life.

Linking her arms with theirs, Miranda brought them up to the big house, where Ryan awaited them on the veranda. Tara was immediately struck by what a good-looking man he was for his age. Dark eyes the same color as his still-thick hair flashed with emotion as he instantly set about defusing the situation.

"I owe you an apology," Ryan said, looking the man he once thought capable of murder straight in the eye.

Jonas offered him his hand in friendship. "If the situation had been reversed, I suppose I would have jumped to the same conclusion you did," he admitted. "Besides, with a gorgeous fiancée and a baby on the way, I just don't think there's going to be enough room in my life for holding unhealthy grudges."

At the pronouncement, a wide, open smile split Ryan's face. "Glad to hear it!" Turning to extend a hand to Tara, he added, "I'm pleased to finally meet you. Miranda's been singing your praises ever since she ran into you the last time you were in town. She certainly was right about you being a real beauty. She maintains that we have you to thank for getting this hardheaded nephew of mine back to give the Fortune family another chance."

Tara blushed, thinking there must be something in the Fortune men's blood that made a girl feel the utter potency in their glance. She found Ryan to be just as friendly and likable as Miranda in his own way. That he cared enough to clean up after his philandering brother Cameron said a great deal about him. That he was man enough to apologize to Jonas for misjudging him spoke volumes, as well.

Scanning the surrounding grounds, Jonas offered a menacing observation. "Considering that whoever's responsible for poisoning you hasn't been caught yet, I wonder if we aren't being a little foolhardy planning a wedding here. Do you mind my asking if you have any protection out here?"

"A personal arsenal for starters," Ryan replied grimly, referring to the many guns he kept locked up in his walk-in vault.

As if worried that Jonas's comment about the lack of security made them all feel vulnerable to a sniper's bullet, Miranda instructed them to come in. "There's someone I want you both to meet," she said.

Ushering them into a large study with a fireplace and a high beamed ceiling, she invited them to sit. Tara and Jonas sank side by side into a luxurious leather couch, which was soft as butter to the touch. The room was tastefully decorated with Spanish blankets, prints, paintings and pottery. Tara was glad to see that wealth hadn't bred all the homeyness out of the place. Though Ryan's home was as different from the one Tara was raised in as the coast was from the hill country, they had something in common. Both exuded a sense of gracious hospitality of which her own parents would have heartily approved.

Tara wondered if Jonas didn't feel rather like the prodigal son, given the way Miranda and Ryan fussed over his return. She tossed him a knowing wink when no one was looking, hoping to allay his fears about being smothered by his new family. As the conversation turned to the subject of the baby, Miranda and Ryan were quick to assure the young couple that all the Fortunes were absolutely wild about children. They also maintained any name chosen would be just fine with them, all the while gently urging the young parents-to-be to at least consider Fortune as the surname.

Rather than dismiss it out of hand, Jonas surprised Tara when he smiled affably and said they'd talk it over when they were alone.

He cleared his throat uncomfortably. "I was hoping to formally thank you and Mary Ellen for your generosity. Ten million dollars is…"

At a loss for words, he threw up his hands as if to say he didn't quite believe it himself.

"Pish posh," Miranda responded as if the gift was no more than some little token she'd put beneath the Christmas tree.

As if eager to dispel any sense of indebtedness Jonas might be feeling, she skillfully switched the topic of conversation.

"Ryan's planning a little holiday get-together in December for some very special friends, and I'm hoping that it won't conflict with any of your plans."

Explaining that they would be honeymooning all of December, Jonas hastened to reiterate his desire to be married as quickly as possible. Being a recipient of the Fortune's generosity himself, he could only imagine the lavishness of the upcoming Christmas party. If the twinkle in his uncle's eye was any indication, the gifts he intended to bestow upon his friends would be nothing short of astonishing.

Turning his attention to the immediate future, Ryan said, "Mary Ellen will be here later. I'm sure you can understand how hard all this has been on her."

Tara supposed so. To discover that your husband had sired at least three children out of wedlock would have to be both personally and socially devastating. The fact that Mary Ellen had actually bequeathed her husband's illegitimate children a substantial portion of his wealth said much about her character.

Jonas and Ryan agreed to leave the wedding arrangements to the women; Jonas cared only that the wedding take place within the week. Although Miranda would have preferred a big do to present the latest members of the Fortune family to the world, the bride-to-be insisted on a small but tasteful ceremony. The basics were already in place. Tara's two brothers were to be groomsmen, and Jonas's half sister her maid of honor. Naturally her father would give her away.

She had already picked out her dress. An off-the-shoulder concoction of imported French silk with opera-style lace gloves and a matching bridal train of impressive length, the gown itself was reminiscent of courtly days when kings spared no coin to bedeck their queens in the most exquisite clothes to be had. Its flowing lines hid the tiny bulge of her stomach. She planned to sweep her hair up in ringlets and hold the shining bulk of it atop her head by a bridal veil encrusted with tiny seed pearls. Around her neck, she was to wear a matching strand of her mother's treasured pearls.

All that was left to plan were the flowers, refreshments and the ceremony itself.

They were in the midst of discussing how best to utilize the gazebo as the focal point of the ceremony when an attractive man appeared in the arched entryway. Miranda's blue eyes opened wide as if to fit more of him into her view. Tara instantly recognized the look. It was the same one she herself gave Jonas. It was the look of a woman in love.

Jumping to her feet, Miranda hastened to introduce the new arrival to her guests.

"Tara, Jonas, this is Daniel Smythe, an old and very dear friend of mine. Daniel, I'd like you to meet the newest members of the Fortune family."

"It's an honor," he said. Urging them not to stand on his account, Daniel proceeded to break the ice with a rueful shake of his head. "Let me be the first one to welcome you to this crazy family. But before you get too comfortable here, I think there are a few things you need to know about the Fortunes that the tabloids don't cover.''

A look of horror crossed Miranda's face. ''Surely we don't need to subject our guests to our dirty laundry,'' she pleaded in that soft Southern drawl designed to melt men's hearts.

But Daniel Smythe was not a man to be dissuaded by such feminine wiles.

''No one would argue that the Fortunes haven't made their share of mistakes, but you've got to give them credit for attempting to remedy them—even if it is years after the fact. An awful lot of wealthy families would do their damnedest to keep your lineage a secret, Jonas. But not the Fortunes. No, sir. This family does everything in their power to rectify their mistakes—even if it means diminishing their wealth, subjecting themselves to scurrilous reporters, exposing themselves to attempted murder in their own homes…or losing the one true love of her life for the sake of honesty.''

Though Daniel addressed his remaining remarks to Jonas, his eyes never left Miranda.

''I think I can safely say that I alone in this room can understand the shock you felt when you discovered that you're part of a family you didn't even know you had. You see, before accepting my proposal of marriage, your beautiful aunt Miranda decided she'd better tell me about the twins I'd fathered but never knew about.''

Miranda bit her lip hard enough to stain her pale lipstick with a drop of bright red blood.

''I seriously thought about turning my back on her and never looking back until I stopped to consider the courage it must have taken for her to disclose that information, knowing full well that she was risking my love for the sake of setting things right. And I realized what a fool I'd be to lose her—again.''

''So I'm here to tell you both that I think you're the luckiest couple alive to be asked to be part of a family like that. A family that's as happy about adding another baby to the family tree as they are about embracing you and your beautiful bride, Jonas. And I'm proud to have you witness my fumbling attempt to become part of this crazy wonderful family myself—if Miranda will still have me, that is.''

She didn't make him wait for her answer.

''I hope you know what a mistake it was to make that lovely speech before witnesses,'' she chided tearfully pulling him into the loving circle of her arms. ''It will make it all the harder to back out that way.''

''No need to worry on that account,'' Daniel assured her. ''Just as soon as all the proper arrangements can be made, I intend to marry the girl I fell in love with all those years ago.'' He corrected himself with a little smile. ''Or rather, the incredible woman she's become.''

Tara dabbed at the tears blurring her vision as Jonas looked at her with newfound insight into the healing power of forgiveness. That this man could accept the challenges that fate placed in his way and let go of his resentments made Jonas think hard about discarding his own. In comparison to Daniel's, his seemed infinitesimally small.

Clearly Tara had been right all along about the importance of family. Though he'd initially agreed to a wedding in Texas just to humor her, the lump in his throat put there by this moving display of affection was suddenly making him susceptible to all kinds of suggestions. Even relocating from San Francisco to a more family-central location. Cupping Tara's chin in one hand, Jonas tilted up her face and deposited a kiss upon lips already swollen by all the attention he'd paid them lately.

Not caring a whit for propriety, he had every intention of lavishing even more attention upon them and the rest of her luscious body just as soon as they were settled in for the evening. He hoped his aunt and uncle didn't object to them sharing a room before the wedding. Whether they did or not, Jonas intended to spend every night for the rest of his life in the same bed with Tara. As far as he was concerned, they were already married in their hearts. A piece of paper wasn't going to make any difference in the way he felt about the woman he held safe in the crook of his arm.

"As much as I love the thought of planning a double wedding, I wouldn't think of undermining your special day," Miranda assured them.

Though both Tara and Jonas assured her that wouldn't be the case, that it would simply double their joy to share in her happiness, it soon became apparent that Miranda was planning the social event of the decade. One could almost see the wheels in her mind turning over endless possibilities.

"We'll invite all the Fortunes, new and old. It will be the biggest celebration this family's ever seen! I know just the right wedding planner, too. Her name is Michelle Guillaire. February should be a convenient time, don't you think? You'll be back from your honeymoon by then, and you'll come, won't you?" Miranda asked.

It was more of a statement than a question.

"Of course we will," Tara hastened to assure her, nudging Jonas gently in the side with an elbow.

Laughing at such wifely tactics, he said, "We wouldn't miss it for the world." However, recalling all the trouble he had gotten into the last time he'd attended a Fortune gathering, he did attach one emphatic stipulation.

"Just make sure somebody else brings the wine," he told them with a self-effacing grin.

* * * * *

This holiday Ryan Fortune has
a special gift
for each of the four people who
helped him in his hour of need.
Each gift will irrevocably alter
these individuals' lives
as they discover true love.
Be sure to watch for

GIFTS OF FORTUNE,

coming only to Silhouette Books
in November 2001.

And now, for a sneak preview
of the first short story
in this holiday collection,
please turn the page.

Chapter 1

The Christmas party was in full swing, with Fortune family members of all ages spilling out of the aptly titled great room, mixing and mingling in the other downstairs rooms. Patriarch Ryan Fortune's home, one of the big houses on the fabled Double Crown Ranch, resembled a Spanish hacienda on the outside. Inside the design was open and airy with one room flowing into another.

Nico Tan-efi stood alone, holding a crystal cup filled with eggnog and studying Ryan Fortune. The tycoon projected a strong presence. He was everyone's focal point. But he was a good listener, which Nico knew from personal experience with the man.

Nico thought of his after-hours hospital visits to Ryan Fortune's bedside as the older man gradually recovered from poisoning.

Their conversations had covered many subjects. One might not expect a middle-aged Texas billionaire and a thirty-two-year-old sheik from the Middle Eastern country of Imarco to have anything in common except the oil business, but Ryan and Nico had found it easy to talk about anything. Women and life, in general and specifically.

"I have an announcement to make." Ryan Fortune's deep voice resonated throughout the great room. "Although I've always been more of a man of action than a philosopher, since the last time we were all together like this, I've had lots of time on my hands to think."

"No doubt getting poisoned tends to make one philosophical, Dad," somebody interjected wryly.

Nico tried to see who it was. If Ryan Fortune was "Dad" to that person, then he, Nico, was a half brother. In fact, he was probably related to all the people at this party, a whole new tribe of brothers, sisters, nieces, nephews, uncles and aunts. His family tree had been irrevocably altered and expanded, though only he was aware of it.

Wait until he told Esme he had yet another brother! Nico smiled. Almost instantly his smile disappeared. This eggnog must be strongly spiked, and as he rarely indulged in alcohol, its effect was hitting him hard and fast. Only that could explain his unexpected forbidden thought of Esme.

His former fiancée was not permitted to slip through the impenetrable fortress guarding his heart and mind. At least not during his conscious daylight hours. It was only late at night as he lay alone in bed and was drifting into sleep that images of Esme broke free.

"I decided to have this party, not only to gather my loved ones together again," Ryan went on in a welcome interruption to Nico's torturous thoughts, "but also to give something back to four special people who did something for me out of the goodness of their hearts. With Christmas just around the corner, tonight seems like an ideal time. Nico Tan-efi, Sebastian Quentin, Jessamine Miller and Dr. Maggie Taylor, will you please all come over here to me? I have a gift for each of you."

Nico approached Ryan, feeling the curious glances of the crowd. He cast a few covert glances of his own at his fellow mysterious-gift recipients. They did likewise, each looking as surprised as he.

Ryan introduced all four and gave a brief summary of what each one had done for him "out of the goodness of their hearts." And then he fixed his penetrating dark eyes on the man he did not know was his own son. "King Nico Tan-efi saved my business reputation last year when some members of the Middle East oil cartel decided it would be good sport to make a fool out of the rancher from Texas. But Nico tipped me off...though there was nothing in it for him to do that for me."

Nico cleared his throat. "Ah, but there was, Ryan. There was our honor as fellow businessmen at stake."

Ryan's eyes misted as he proceeded to hand out the special gifts to the chosen four.

Nico opened his own beautifully wrapped gift box a while later in Ryan's study, as the older man looked on, his expression eager with anticipation. Nico snapped open a satin-lined box that held a masculine gold ring with a distinctive double-crown inlay. He stared at it, wide-eyed.

"This ring is not merely a sentimental piece of jewelry, Nico. It has power, a kind of mystical power that makes true love survive. And since you remind me of myself in many ways, you will need this ring, just as I needed it. I might as well admit this to you. I know all about what happened between you and Esme Bakkar.''

Nico froze. Just the sound of her name was enough to send a bolt of pain through him.

''Circumstances have changed since you last saw Esme, Nico. There is no longer danger of a revolt in Imarco. You've proved your mettle. Now it's time to win Esme back. And with the power of this ring you will, because she is your true love.''

FORTUNES OF TEXAS: THE LOST HEIRS
Fortune Family Tree

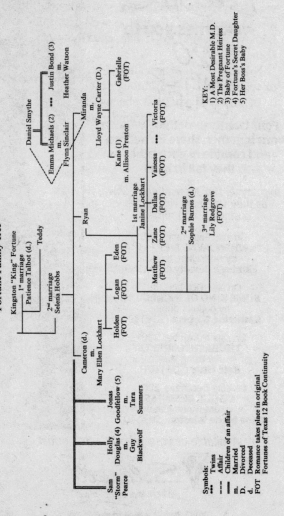

Symbols:
- ••• Twins
- --- Affair
- ▬ Children of an affair
- m. Married
- D. Divorced
- d. Deceased
- FOT Romance takes place in original Fortunes of Texas 12 Book Continuity

KEY:
1) A Most Desirable M.D.
2) The Pregnant Heiress
3) Baby of Fortune
4) Fortune's Secret Daughter
5) Her Boss's Baby

CALL THE ONES YOU LOVE OVER THE HOLIDAYS!

Save $25 off future book purchases when you buy any four Harlequin® or Silhouette® books in October, November and December 2001,

PLUS

receive a phone card good for 15 minutes of long-distance calls to anyone you want in North America!

WHAT AN INCREDIBLE DEAL!

Just fill out this form and attach 4 proofs of purchase (cash register receipts) from October, November and December 2001 books, and Harlequin Books will send you a coupon booklet worth a total savings of $25 off future purchases of Harlequin® and Silhouette® books, AND a 15-minute phone card to call the ones you love, anywhere in North America.

Please send this form, along with your cash register receipts
as proofs of purchase, to:
In the USA: Harlequin Books, P.O. Box 9057, Buffalo, NY 14269-9057
In Canada: Harlequin Books, P.O. Box 622, Fort Erie, Ontario L2A 5X3
Cash register receipts must be dated no later than December 31, 2001.
Limit of 1 coupon booklet and phone card per household.
Please allow 4-6 weeks for delivery.

I accept your offer! Please send me my coupon booklet and a 15-minute phone card:

Name: _____

Address: _____ City: _____

State/Prov.: _____ Zip/Postal Code: _____

Account Number (if available): _____

---

097 KJB DAGL
PHQ4012